Vampire

Dead-tective

Related Series by Mac Flynn

Dead-tective Series
Vampire Soul

Vampire Dead-tective

Dead-tective Book One

Mac Flynn

All names, places, and events depicted in this book are fictional and products of the author's imagination.

No part of this publication may be reproduced, stored in a retrieval system, converted to another format, or transmitted in any form without explicit, written permission from the publisher of this work. For information regarding redistribution or to contact the author, write to the publisher at the following address.

Crescent Moon Studios, Inc.
P.O. Box 1531
Prosser, WA 99350

Website: www.macflynn.com
Email: mac@macflynn.com

ISBN / EAN-13: 978-1517783204

First Edition

Chapter 1

We weren't really a thing. Well, at least not usually. We were just really good friends with the occasional benefits. That's why we shared an apartment, but not a life. That is, until he was killed. Actually, that's not true. He wasn't killed, he was murdered.

But let me start from the top. My name is Liz Stokes, and I was a normal office girl working at a normal day job that normally paid the bills. The only weird part about my life was my roommate for my normal apartment. His name was Timothy Hamilton, and he was, well, eccentric. We stumbled into each other one autumn's evening five years ago. I was taking a walk, he was laying in some bushes with so many bruises over his body he looked like Barney the Dinosaur. I don't like watching stupid animals suffer, so I helped him back to my apartment and like most strays he stayed there.

That's how I learned how weird were his habits. Timothy was a night owl who dragged himself in at early hours of the morning and often collapsed on the couch. That was where I usually found him, if I found him at all. Sometimes he would leave for a few days and come back to crash for a few more days. Other times he would be awake at all hours of the day thanks to a gallon of coffee and superhuman perseverance. I'm sure you're asking why he had such strange hours, and that was because of his job. He told me he was a kind of consultant, and when I found him he'd just had some bad luck in a mediation. That was how he was able to pay for his half of the apartment rent. I suggested a change of occupation, but he argued that he'd been doing it for so long he didn't have any other skills.

Which now brings us to the man himself. Timothy was old-fashioned in his mannerisms. He'd open doors for me and sweep off invisible hats when we met. I have to admit it made me feel special, and that's why we were sometimes more than just roommates.

With all his gallant manners and cute eccentricities there was one thing about him I couldn't stand, and that was his partner, Vincent. Vincent was tall, pale, and unfriendly. He wore a black overcoat with a duster, and had a faded black fedora. It made him dashingly handsome, but I couldn't get past his cold manner and eyes. I hoped he wasn't the face of their Public Relations department.

The first time I met Vincent Timothy had us shake hands, or tried to have us shake hands. I held out mine, but Vincent just sneered and turned away. Timothy brought him over to the apartment only a few more times before he noticed Vincent and I didn't hit it off, and then the visits stopped.

There was one final weird thing about Timothy that happened shortly after we agreed to share the apartment. He took me aside and handed me a small metal box. "If you ever find out something's happened to me then you take this box and follow the instructions, okay?"

"Like what?" I'd asked him.

He shook his head. "You'll know when it happens, but don't hesitate to follow the instructions inside. Got it?" He was so strange that I took the whole thing as a joke and stuffed the box under my bed. How wrong I was, and how I wished I would have better enjoyed the time we had together.

Those halcyon days of strange hours with my strange roommate came to an abrupt end three years after we met. It was a Friday afternoon and I was just finishing up my work at the office. It was one of those cubicle-filled places where the hum of the hive was really the water cooler in need of repair. I clicked and clacked through the last few sentences of a document I was typing for a boss who had an aversion to anything related to keyboards.

I clacked the last word, leaned back and groaned as I stretched. "And that completes another riveting day of office work," I mused.

A head peeked over one wall of my prison. It was a fellow prisoner by the name of Jeremy who I suspected had a crush on me. Maybe it was the occasional flower on my desk or the longing smile on his face. I would have encouraged it if I felt the same way, but I couldn't get past how ever-present he was around me. If we would have started dating I imagined he would have been one of those ever-texting boyfriends asking me where I was and who I was with. Not a healthy relationship.

"Have any plans for the weekend?" he asked me.

"None that I know of, and I'm just fine with that," I replied, seeking to discourage any plans he might have had for me.

His smile slipped a little. Apparently I'd warded off trouble in the nick of time. "I see. I was sort of hoping that we could go out to see a movie."

I sighed and straightened in my chair. "Not this weekend. Nothing's playing that I want to see and I might have to nuke my apartment to clean it." I was a little behind on my dusting, dish cleaning, vacuuming, mopping, and anything else that involved cleaning and the ending of 'ing.' "It may take me until next year to get everything done."

Jeremy snorted. "Well, good luck," he replied, and slipped out of sight.

Thus ended that Friday afternoon. I returned to the apartment and found that Timothy wasn't home. As I said before that wasn't so unusual except that he'd been gone for nearly a week. I wondered at what point I needed to call the police and submit a missing person report when there was a knock on the door.

I looked through the peephole and saw it was a uniformed officer. That was service for you. I opened the door. "Can I help you?" I asked him.

He held up a wallet with a badge, but flipped it back inside his coat before I caught a good look at it. "Officer Sutton with the Third Precinct. Is this the residence of Timothy Hamilton?"

My heart picked up speed. "Yeah, why?"

"I'm afraid something's happened to him. Are you related to him?"

Horrible images and possibilities passed through my mind. "No, I'm just his roommate. What's happened to him?"

"Mr. Hamilton's been murdered. His body was found a few hours ago along the river." My mouth dropped open and I stumbled back. The officer stepped inside and caught me. He helped me over to the couch where I sat down in numb disbelief. "I'm sorry about this, but if you could come down to the station we're going to need a statement from you."

"What? Oh, yes, of course." I mechanically stood and stumbled toward my room. "Just let me change and get a coat." I was still in my uncomfortable work clothes.

"Certainly," the officer kindly agreed.

I went into my room and closed the door behind me. That's when the full force of the officer's words hit me, and I burst into uncontrollable sobs. I slid onto the floor in a blubbering mass of tears and denial. Timothy, my Timothy, was dead. I didn't want to believe that he was gone, that something horrible had happened to him and I wouldn't see him again.

My eyes widened. "Something happened to him. . ." I softly repeated aloud. Those were the words he'd used when he handed me that box all those years ago. Sitting as I was I could see under my bed and the box stared back at me. Hope surged inside me that maybe this was some cruel joke of his, and that maybe the box held the punchline. I quickly crawled over to it and noticed there were fresh fingerprints on the dusty top. I fumbled with the clasp and the top popped open. Inside was a slip of paper and a ring I'd seen Timothy wear constantly. He must have put the ring in the box just before he went off to get himself-well, get himself in trouble.

My hands shook as I opened the paper which turned out to be a note.

Dear Liz,

If you're reading this then either you're sneaking a peek when you shouldn't or something's happened to me. If the former, then put this note back and don't look at it until the latter happens. If something really has happened to me then you're in danger.

My heart stopped beating for a moment, but I continued reading.

5

I'm sorry I couldn't explain all of this while I was alive, but I didn't want you to get involved. With my probable death you're knee-deep in my troubles, and I'm sorry for what you need to do, but know that it's the only thing you can do. Take this ring to the address at the bottom of this letter and wait inside the warehouse until after dark. No matter what, even if someone you trust comes to get you, you have to get to that warehouse. If you're reading this at night then put on the ring and pray. Pray for me, too, okay?

Love, Timothy

I covered my mouth to stifle my sobs. He really was dead, and through this letter he'd warned me about some unknown danger. I jumped when there was a loud knock on the door. "Miss, are you all right?" the officer called to me.

"I-I'm fine, just-" I paused and glanced down at the letter. Timothy instructed me to hurry to the warehouse and the sun was even now setting. I glanced around my room and noticed the window and the fire escape. I could get down that and drive to the warehouse-

Wait a minute, why the hell was I running from an officer? All he wanted to do was take me down to the station to give a statement. Still, Timothy's note made me suspicious, and I snuck over to the door. I opened it a crack and glanced at the officer. He was working the apartment over like a pro burglar as he stuck his hands and head into every hole and corner. Nothing too unusual about that. He was probably getting a head start on the investigation.

I slipped on my coat, stuffed the letter and ring into a pocket, and stepped out of my room. "I'm ready," I announced to him.

The officer jumped, grabbed his gun, and swung around with the barrel pointed at me. I jumped backwards and my back hit the wall beside my bedroom door. He smiled and re-holstered his weapon. "Sorry about that. It's a habit of mine."

"T-that's a bad habit," I commented. Even without Timothy's instructions ringing in my mind I didn't want to go with a guy that had such an itchy trigger finger.

"No harm done," he insisted. He turned to the front door, paused, and turned back to me. "Oh, did you happen to know where Timothy kept a ring?" he asked me.

My heart picked up speed. "N-no, why?"

"We suspect he stole some jewelery, and that's part of the missing stash," he told me.

I unconsciously reached into my pocket and clutched the ring. I faked astonishment. "A jewel thief? When'd he steal it?"

"Um, about two years ago, but that's not important. Let's get you down to the station for the questioning, and then we'll get you back here." That was actually very important to me because I'd seen Timothy with the ring far longer than two years. The officer was lying, and I didn't want to find out why.

Chapter 2

I obediently followed him out into the hall and downstairs to the lobby where I glanced around looking for some chance to get away. My eyes fell on the public restrooms, and I stopped and pointed at them. "I need to go to the bathroom."

He turned to me with a deep frown. "Can't you hold it?"

I shook my head. "No, but this won't take more than a minute."

Before he could argue I rushed into the girl's bathroom, leaned against one of the stalls and clutched at my heart. Something was seriously wrong here, and Timothy's letter proved he knew I'd be in danger. The big problem I had was what was dangerous and what was safe. Timothy wanted me to go to the warehouse, and the cop wanted me to go to the precinct. As a law-abiding citizen I wanted to go to the station, but the officer lied to me about Timothy's ring. I pulled out the paper and ring from my pocket. Who was I going to believe me, my dead friend or a cop I'd never met who'd already lied to me?

Yeah, not much of a contest there. If the cop really did just want to question me he could pick me up later. Right now I had a warehouse to get to, so I looked around the bathroom and saw a ventilation window at the end of the stalls. It was only four feet above the floor and I wasn't that fat, so I stuffed the letter back into my pocket and, for safety's sake, put the ring on my finger and went over to the window.

I hefted myself up over the sill and pulled myself through the open, angled window. I was nearly out when I heard a knock on the door. "You almost done?" the officer shouted.

"Almost!" I shouted back. Unfortunately, because my head stuck out of the building my voice sounded off, and that alerted the cop. He rushed into the room just as I slipped my legs through.

"Hey, stop!" He dashed over to the window, but I climbed to my feet and sprinted down the alley toward the street.

I dashed around the corner and saw my car parked on the curb. Unfortunately, I skidded to a stop when I noticed the police car and the cop's partner sitting inside. I did an about-face in the other direction and was halfway down the alley when I heard shouts from the front of the building and glanced over my shoulder. Two cops raced after me, one of them being Officer Sutton. Fortunately I was in better shape than them, and I had fear and adrenaline to get me going.

I lost them a few blocks down, and stopped for a breather in an alley. "I. . .am. . .so. . .dead," I gasped. I'd just ditched a couple of cops, and they were going to tell all their uniformed friends about me. I pulled out the letter from Timothy and sighed. "I hope you're right about this, Tim," I whispered.

I kept in the shadows of the alleys and my heart skipped a few beats whenever I heard the sirens of a police car. The address at the bottom of the letter led me to the river and a row of old, rectangular, abandoned warehouses that had been built on a small island a hundred yards out on the water. The sunlight was nearly gone and a cold wind from the water swept over me. I shuddered and hurried across a narrow paved road that crossed the water and led up to a chain-link gate and fence. The entire island was surrounded by the fence, and the top had coils of barbed wire. Besides the warehouses there were rotten crates and pallets, and an old guardhouse stood behind the gate.

A narrow patch of gravel ran along either side of the fence, and it took me a few minutes to find a hole beneath the fence that had been made by wild dogs and stupid kids. I wiggled my way through the loose gravel to the other side and I followed the peeled numbers on the buildings until I found the right warehouse. They ran lengthwise with the bank, and the one I was looking for was the one closest to the far-off shore. I looked over the broken window panes and the metal, and a sense of dread flooded over me. This place looked haunted, and the dim light didn't comfort me.

I sighed and tried the knob. It was unlocked, so I stepped inside and looked around. There was just enough light for me to see that the place was full of broken crates stacked well over my head. They created a maze of wood that wound its way to the rear of the building. I moved through them and twenty yards from the door I found a space where the maze walls parted. The crates were arranged like a bench around a single long rectangular box. On the box was a deck of cards, a propane lantern, and a box of matches.

I eagerly lit the lamp and sat down on the makeshift bench in front of the long box. The air inside the warehouse was dank and cool, and I rubbed my arms to comfort and warm me. Outside the sun finished setting and the world was enveloped in darkness. To pass the time I pulled out the letter and reread the contents. I really wished Tim would have put in a few more specifics about what I was supposed to be waiting for.

I didn't have long to wait. As I sat reading the letter the light from the lamp shuddered. I lowered the letter and glared at the lantern. The flame was strong and unwavering, but then it jiggled again. That's when I realized it wasn't the light flickering but the entire lantern. My eyes widened when the lid of the long box moved. I grabbed the lantern and jumped back just as the lid flew off. A dark figure arose from the box, and I held out the lantern toward it.

My eyes widened when they fell on Vincent, and he didn't look happy to see me. "What are you doing here?" he demanded to know.

What the hell had he been doing in there? What the hell had he been doing in the box? "I-I-" I stuttered.

Vincent swooped toward me with such speed that before I knew it the lantern and letter were slapped from my hands. The paper fluttered to the ground and the lantern clattered to the hard floor, but remained lit. I shrieked when he shoved his pale face into mine, and in the lantern light his teeth looked unnaturally long.

"What are you doing here?" he growled.

I stumbled backward and my back hit a tower of crates. "T-Tim told me to come here. Something happened to him," I replied.

Vincent straightened and raised an eyebrow. "What happened?"

"H-he was murdered," I told him.

Vincent's eyes widened and he hurriedly placed his hand over his chest. Whatever he felt it made his thin mouth turn up in a twisted grin. "So he's dead at last? How wonderful."

"Wonderful?" I gasped. After fleeing from cops and sneaking around half the city to find this place this psycho from the box was the one I'd been waiting to meet? I cursed Tim for his stupidity in leading me here, but I wouldn't let anybody celebrate his death. My hands balled into fists and I marched up to Vincent. "Tim's dead, you idiot! Don't you know what that means?"

"Yes, but you don't." Vincent lunged for me and his hands grasped my shoulders. He slammed me back against the crates with such force that their heavy frames rattled and the air was knocked from my lungs.

I saw stars, but through those stars I noticed Vincent's eyes burned with an unnatural light. "What the hell are you doing?" I exclaimed.

Vincent grinned and leaned forward to brush his nose against my cheek. I shuddered at the contact of his cold skin against mine. His nostrils flared. "The human beauty is so fragile. A single bullet and your light is extinguished." I flinched when one of his hands slid up my thigh and came to rest on my waist. He pressed his body against mine, pinning me to the crates. "You have such beauty, but I won't save it for eternity."

"W-what are you talking about?" I breathed. "Tim just told me to come here and-"

I jumped when Vincent tightened his grasp on my shoulders. My bones creaked under the strain. "Tim was an idiot, and I will thank him for these many years of slavery by draining you of every last drop of blood," he whispered. My heart skipped a beat and I wiggled in his grasp, but he was strong, unbelievably strong. His eyes traveled down to my neck, and then back up to my wide, scared eyes. "Wouldn't that be fitting revenge?" he mused. He was toying with me like a cat with a mouse. His amusement vanished when he glanced at my left hand. His eyes widened in fury and fear, and he pulled his face away from mine. "What are you doing with that?" he growled. I didn't know what he was talking about until I remembered the ring on my finger. "Take it off!" he demanded as one of his hands swept down to grab the ring.

A bright, white light erupted from the ring. The heat was so intense I could feel the width of the narrow band etch into my finger. Vincent screamed in agony and I was released from his iron grasp. I dropped to the ground and raised myself up on my side in time to watch Vincent stumble backward. He clutched at his left hand where another intense light emanated. I realized he wore the same ring as mine. A few yards from me he collapsed to his knees and the light swallowed him. My only thought was to get the ring off before the same happened to me, so I grasped the ring in my hand and pulled. The ring slowly slid across my finger, and in the background of my struggle Vincent cried out in horrible pain. The moment the ring slipped off my finger the light vanished, but I was left with a searing pain in my finger. The ring dropped onto the ground and rolled away. I glanced down at my quivering hand and saw a few engraved letters on my skin fade into my body.

I slumped against the crate wall and my breaths came out in haggard gasps. I heard Vincent groan, and I glanced over to where he lay. He was huddled in a tight, quivering ball, but he soon pulled himself from his cocoon and turned to face me. His eyes were full of a confusing mix of hate, anger, and fear. He struggled to his feet, but I was as weak as a lamb. I could do nothing but sit there as he towered over me.

I expected him to attack me again, but instead his arms dropped to his sides and a sick smirk slid onto his lips. "So that's what he planned," he hoarsely whispered. "Smart boy."

Chapter 3

"Tim?" I croaked.

Vincent's reply was to shuffle toward me, and I pressed myself against the crate. When he reached me he knelt down on one knee and looked me over. I cringed and prepared for death, but he did nothing. He only stared at me with those unblinking, intense eyes.

His inaction made me mad. I was tired of being the mouse. "If you're going to kill me then do it," I demanded.

"I wish I could," he quipped.

I blinked in bewilderment. "But you-"

"The circumstances have changed, and so have both of us," he interrupted. "What did Timothy tell you about our relationship?"

The change in subject was so sudden that I habitually shrugged. My whole body ached with the motion. "He said you were partners."

Vincent chuckled. "Is that what he told you? That we were some sort of a team? All for one and one for all?" I cringed, but nodded. He scoffed and his face twisted into disgust. "We were nothing of the sort." That was all I needed to hear from this psychopath. I slowly scooted along the floor, but Vincent slammed a hand against the crate next to my head that arrested my escape. "You're to go nowhere," he told me.

I frowned. "If you're not going to kill me then what are you going to do to me?" I asked him.

"I'm going to protect you." I raised a doubtful eyebrow, and he impatiently sighed. "You're a slow one, aren't you? Have you even figured out what I am?"

"A psychopath?" I guessed.

He smirked. "True, but that doesn't describe my species."

"I just want to-ah!" A spasm of pain shot through my sore hand. I doubled over and clutched at my shivering fingers. Vincent grabbed my shoulders and held me still. I grit my teeth and raised my head to look at him. "What's going on?" I asked him.

"The union isn't finished yet. Where is the ring?" he asked me. My eyes traveled to the fallen lantern. The ring had rolled up beside the glass casing around the flame. Vincent followed my gaze, and he left me to snatch the ring and return. "Put this back on," he instructed me as he held out the ring. I squished against the crate and shook my head. I wasn't going through that pain again. He sneered at me and shoved the ring into my palm. "Put it-"

His insistence was interrupted by the sound of guns outside the warehouse. Bullets penetrated the thin walls of the old building and shot over our heads. I swung my arms over my head and ducked down. Vincent threw himself over me and pressed me to the floor. He stuck his head close to mine and his long teeth looked impossibly sharp. "Put on the ring or we're both dead!" he snapped.

I was too panicked to argue, and hurriedly slipped the ring onto my finger. I clutched my hand as pain shot out from the band of metal and into my body. Vincent clenched his teeth and I heard his stifled cries as his pain mirrored mine. The gunfire outside was replaced by a more hideous sound of a large wolf howling. I heard the front door being ripped off its hinges and tossed aside. Clawed feet clinked quickly along the hard floor, and through the pain of the ring I imagined a far worse death than the one promised by Vincent. I feared I would be torn apart by some bloodthirsty hound. How wrong I was.

The clinking claws came closer and rounded the corner of a nearby crate stack. I turned my head and my eyes widened when, by the light of the dim lantern, I beheld not a large dog, but a wolf creature larger than a man. It spotted us and raised itself onto its hind legs. The wolf thing tipped its head back and howled. The awful noise echoed through the metallic building and sent a shiver through my body. It dropped back down on all four legs and raced toward us.

Vincent flew off me and jumped between the monster and me. When the beast was a foot from him Vincent kicked out a leg in a circular motion and knocked the monster's front legs out from under it. The wolf crashed head-first into the hard floor and slid into the crate of boxes behind me. The wooden boxes toppled over him. I crawled away, but the pain wracked my body so badly that I couldn't find the strength to stand.

Vincent grabbed one of the crates and tore a long, jagged steak from the wood. The wolf beast burst from the crates and howled in rage. Its golden eyes fell on me, and I screamed when it lunged at me. Vincent tackled the beast from the side and the pair of them rolled away from me. I backed up and my hand knocked into something hard but light. It was the lantern. I grabbed the lantern and swung it in front of me to watch the tussle.

The beast righted itself and dove at Vincent, but he was too fast and dodged the thing's claws. Vincent slipped behind the wolf and raised the stake to plunge the weapon into the creature's back.   The beast turned the tables by using Vincent's trick of round-kicking a leg to knock him off his feet.   Vincent fell hard on his back, and the beast turned around to tear Vincent to pieces.   I thought fast and threw the lantern at the beast's back.   The flame hit the thing's fur and caught the hair on fire.

The creature screamed and waved its arms in a futile attempt to to reach back and extinguish the flames.   Vincent grabbed the stake and jabbed it into the creature's chest.   The wolf released a long, terrible howl before it fell over dead. The fur continued to burn, and by its light I watched the thing transform from a furry demon to a barely-clothed man. Once the transformation was complete the fire was extinguished from the no-longer existing hair on his back.   I was completely enveloped in darkness, still wracked with pain, and alone with Vincent.

I shrieked when I felt myself lifted into a pair of strong arms.   "Quiet," Vincent ordered me.   He held me against his chest and dashed away from the front door and through the maze of crates.   We quickly reached the rear, and he turned and slammed his back into a heavy metal door that led outside.   I was grateful to be able to see where we were going.

That is, until Vincent raced along the rear of the other warehouses.   His speed was impossibly fast for a human.   The ground sped by in a flurry of rocks, broken pieces of glass, and trash, and in a few seconds we covered a distance that would have taken me at least a minute to cross.   I tried to free myself and get off this horrible ride, but he only pressed me harder to his chest.   "Don't move," he growled.

I stiffened and obeyed his command, especially when I saw how many cars and people stood in front of the warehouses. There were at least half a dozen cars and twice that number of men dressed in black suits. They had dark sunglasses over their eyes, and all of them were armed. Half of them stood at the entrance to the end warehouse, but the other half was spread out between the gate and where we stood behind the center warehouse. Vincent crept up to the front of the warehouse where stood a few crates, but any further and we'd be seen.

We heard shouts from our former warehouse. The body of the wolf man had been discovered. The men who stood in front of the gate glanced in that direction, and Vincent took advantage of their distraction. He shot out of our hiding spot behind a few crates and raced to the gate. The chain-link gate was shut, but that didn't slow him down. The men in sunglasses noticed our escape and turned their guns on us. Shots rang out and bullets whizzed by our heads. Their aim must have been as bad as a Storm Trooper's because they didn't hit Vincent. At least, he didn't slow down, but my body felt pricked by dozens of pins. Then something hot dug into my shoulder as one of the men hit their mark, me. The bullet flew through my shoulder and my blood soaked my shirt.

We were ten yards from the gate when Vincent leapt up into the air. The momentum of his prodigious speed flew us over the top of the barbed wire and onto the other side. He landed with a crunch on the pavement. The closed gate slowed down our pursuers and gave us a head-start down the river road. We entered the asphalt jungle before their cars left the warehouse island, and Vincent didn't have any trouble losing them in the maze of dark alleys and narrow, dingy streets.

Regardless of the danger I was glad when he stopped us in an alley that showed off a splendid mix of dankness and squalor. My wound still bled and the pain was nearly as bad as what the ring had caused. I cried out when he set me down a little too hard against a brick wall. "Quiet," he commanded.

I glared at him. "Quiet? There's a god damn bullet hole in my shoulder!" I snapped back at him.

Vincent ignored my whining and ripped open my bloodied shirt sleeve. The blood had dribbled down my arm and chest, and covered half my body. I expected him to wrap it with the torn sleeve, but Vincent only stared unblinkingly at the wound. "Vincent?" I asked him. He didn't reply and I nervously shifted beneath his unwavering gaze. His hand shot out and grabbed my shoulder to hold me still. My eyes caught sight of his clothes and for the first time I noticed it was riddled with bullet hole. Those guys in suits hadn't missed, they'd shot him full of lead. He shouldn't have been alive, much less holding me down. My heart raced as I remembered how he'd earlier threatened to kill me. Vincent's sharp teeth gleaned in the weak light of the night, but his pallor stood out in the dark shadows of the alley. He looked like a creature of the night, like a- "Vampire!" I gasped.

Vincent lunged forward and buried his teeth into my shoulder. I yelped and tried to jerk away, but he held me tight. The initial pain of his penetration melted away and was replaced with a sensual pleasure that spread out from my shoulder. My eyes widened as my body heated, and liquid pooled between my legs. I gasped for air and my face flushed with the creeping need that flooded over my body.

My hot need was slowly replaced with lethargy as I felt Vincent pull my blood from my body. My head lulled to one side and I couldn't keep my eyes open. I thought I would lose consciousness, but a bright light shot through my closed eyelids. The brilliance burned with the intensity of the sun, and reawakened my mind and body. I heard Vincent cry out and opened my eyes in time to see him stumble to the opposite side of the alley. He hissed and snarled at my hand, and I saw that the ring on my finger was the source of the light.

However, it wasn't the only source. His own finger was lit with the same light. He clutched onto his hand and ground his long, sharp fangs together to stifle his cries of pain. His light pulsed and stretched out into a long, thin beam of light that wound its way up toward the sky. It stretched over the distance of the alley and connected with my ring. My eyes shot open and I gasped when I felt an enormous amount of strength enter my body through the beam of light. The lethargy vanished, replaced by an energy that made me feel like I was on a thousand energy drinks, and they were all working.

Vincent screamed and fell to his knees. His face turned a ghastly white and the flesh seemed to shrink and shrivel from his bones. For all his psychotic antics I felt sorry for him. The moment the emotion rose up inside me the light connecting us vanished. The world slipped back into the darkness of night. The energy in my body lessened, but the pain from my wound was gone. When I glanced at my shoulder I realized that the wound had disappeared. All that remained was the mess of blood.

Chapter 4

I heard a groan and turned my head to Vincent's dark shape on the opposite side of the alley. He still sat on his legs and his body shook with a violent tremor. A hoarse chuckle slipped from of his pale lips. "Quick learner, girl, but you nearly killed us both," he whispered.

His weakened state and my healthy state emboldened me, and I scowled at him. "Me kill us? You were the one sucking me dry," I shot back.

"Merely a survival instinct," he argued.

"That nearly killed us both?" I pointed out.

Vincent stumbled to his feet and I scuttled to mine. If he wanted to try his luck with me again then he was going to have to catch me first. "It was necessary to finish the connection between us."

I blinked. "Come again?"

He straightened and winced when his back erupted like a string of firecrackers. "I mean what I mean. We are connected."

"I got that part." I paused, furrowed my brow, and shook my head. "Actually, I didn't get that part. What are you talking about?"

He held up his left hand and showed off the ring that was identical to mine. "These pieces of jewelery were forged with more than metal. They were infused with the blood of an ancient vampire and a spiritually strong human. When a vampire and a human wear them they become bonded to one another. If one feels pain, the other will feel an echo of that pain. If one dies, the other dies."

I held up my hands in front of me. "Wait a minute. If what you're saying is true, and it sounds Cracker Box crazy, then you really are a vampire?"

"Yes."

"And if you tried to kill me you'd get hurt?" I guessed.

"Yes."

"And you're an ass?"

"No."

I shrugged. "I thought I'd try."

"Very amusing." His face was as funny as the grave. "But we don't-"

"Wait a minute." I held up my own ring. "If Tim had this ring and he's dead, how come you aren't dead?" I wondered.

"He wasn't wearing the ring at the time of his death. Instead we find it on you," Vincent pointed out.

"Why would he take it off? Better yet, *how* did he take it off?"

"I do not know, but we have more immediate problems," he reminded me.

I frowned. "Yeah, you're right. Those guys might find us again. I gotta get to the cops and-"

"-and tell them what?" Vincent asked me. "You escaped from men in black suits who had a werewolf in their employ and were saved by a vampire?"

I scowled at him. "I have to tell somebody about this. It's too big for me."

Vincent frowned and tilted his nose up in disdain. "There is one person in this world who would be interested in what you have to say."

"And who might that be, Count Chocula?"

"Frederick Batholomew."

"That's a mouthful."

"His mouth is certainly a problem."

"Why do we need to go to this person rather than somebody who might at least give me protection?" I asked him.

"I am your protection, and Batholomew has other uses."

I looked over the psychotic vampire and cringed against the brick wall behind me. "Hell no are you my protection. You've tried to kill me twice in twenty minutes, and for me that's a record for assassination attempts on my life."

"I am satiated, and our bond is complete. You have nothing left to fear from me," he replied.

I wasn't comforted. "Uh-huh, so you're supposed to protect me like you protected Tim?" I countered.

Vincent's eyes narrowed. "A mere oversight on his part. If he had refrained from trouble during the day then I would have been of use to him."

"Great, so you're only useful for what? Twelve hours in a twenty-four hour day?" I remarked. "Or do vampires not have to sleep and you were just napping in that wooden box I found you in?"

"My body may need to rest during the day, but my powers are yours." He nodded at the ring. "That will offer you all the powers you need. Tim forsook the powers by giving you that ring."

I paused and furrowed my brow. "Wait, so during the day I'm kind of like a vampire?"

"Yes."

"But without that whole sun-burning thing?"

"Perhaps your incessant questions are better directed at Batholomew," Vincent suggested.

"I haven't agreed to go with you to him," I countered. Vincent stalked over to me. I tried to slide away, but he grabbed my arm and swung me into his arms like before. "Hey! Let me down! I can walk!"

"Not as fast as me."

I yelped when he took off down the road, carrying me at warp speed to another adventure.

I grasped onto his arms as we sped through city blocks like they were standing still. Actually, they were standing still, but we were still going really fast. I did notice we weren't going as fast as we had on our escape from Warehouse Island. Still, by the time Vincent put on the brakes we were several miles from the river, and for me we were several blocks from any familiar area. All around us were old factory buildings, hulking skeletons of industrialization with broken windows for eyes and gaping doors for mouths. The only living things besides me and-well, just me, were a few stray cats. There weren't even any streetlights to help me see into the streets that wound their way around the large structures. The only open spot to see the stars lay behind us, and that was just a large loading and unloading area for all the goods they used to manufacture.

Vincent opened his arms and dropped me onto the road. I yelped when I hit the pavement, and rubbed my sore posterity as I scowled up at him. "Do you mind being more careful next time?" I snapped at him.

"I would," he coolly replied.

"Thanks, I appreciate it."

Vincent ignored my snark and walked over to one of the buildings that actually had a pair of steel doors that were closed. He pushed them open and revealed what I expected, a mad scientist's laboratory filled with crazy-looking machines and bright, flashing lights. Wait, what?

I scrambled to my feet and gaped at the scene. "What the hell-?" I breathed out.

"Follow me," Vincent ordered. He stepped inside and the doors began to close behind him.

I hurried in after him and just barely missed a free, and painful, hip tucking procedure. My mouth was still agape as Vincent led me into the bowels of the science that bubbled, boiled, fizzed, and popped around me. There were vials of questionable goop against the left wall and the right wall was covered with diagrams, papers, graphs, sketches, doodles, and equations. The center floor was filled to overflowing with machines I could only guess at what they did, and others I didn't want to get that far with their purpose.

Vincent was unfazed by the weirdness around us and took me to the rear of the factory floor. In the center against the back wall sat a desk, and at the desk sat a strange little man. He had long white hair that was tied in a tail and ran down his back. The man wore a white lab coat that was stained with all the colors of the rainbow and others that didn't suggest anything that pretty. He had a long white mustache with pointed ends, and heavy eyebrows that covered the upper halves of his eyes. I placed his age somewhere between geriatric and Jurassic. He was hunched over a paper furiously writing away by the light of a simple desk lamp.

Vincent walked up to the desk, but I lingered a few yards back beside a tall spire that was either a gumball machine or a torture device. The old man didn't lift his head when he spoke up. "What are you doing here, and with a girl,

25

no less? Did you take a bite out of your partner and pick up a new bride?" the old man quipped.

"Tim is dead," Vincent calmly replied.

The man's head snapped up and those bushy eyebrows crashed down. "Dead? Then why aren't I dancing over your dust?"

"Because he passed the ring on before he died." Vincent half turned and gestured to me. "This girl now has the ring."

The old man, who I realized must be the legendary Frederick Batholomew, turned his eyes on me. I nervously smiled and gave a small wave. "Um, hi," I replied.

Batholomew stood so quickly that his wooden chair toppled over. He scurried around the desk up to me and snatched my left hand from my side. His eyes looked over the ring on my finger, and his face fell. "By God, it is," he muttered. He turned to Vincent. "What happened?"

Vincent shrugged. "He was killed because he didn't wear the ring. Perhaps he wanted to accessorize."

The old man scoffed. "Tim wasn't that foolish. He must have had a reason for giving this girl the ring."

"He didn't give it to me," I spoke up. The men turned to me with interested expressions, and I shrank from their intense gazes. "That is, he just kind of left it in a box under my bed. He said if something happened to him I needed to take it and go to some warehouse."

"Our headquarters, or they were before this foolish woman led a werewolf to it," Vincent explained.

I glared at him. "I didn't lead anybody to it! I just followed what I was supposed to do on Tim's letter."

Batholomew raised an eyebrow. "Letter? May I see this letter?"

I patted myself down and my face paled. "I think I lost it."

"I have it," Vincent spoke up. He pulled the letter from inside his jacket, but he stuffed it back in the inner pocket when Batholomew grabbed for it. "This is between the two of us," he insisted, nodding at me.

"I think as Tim's closest friend and ally I have as much right to see his last words as anyone else," Batholomew argued. I got the feeling these two didn't get along.

"Um, boys?" I spoke up. They glanced back at me, but this time I wasn't cowed by their eyes. "Could I have *my* letter back? And could somebody please explain to me what the hell is going on here?"

Batholomew frowned and his eyes dodged over to Vincent. "How much does she know?"

"Enough to survive," Vincent replied.

"And hold a job!" I protested.

"As I said, enough to survive," he repeated.

"What do you know about this oaf here?" Batholomew asked me as he nodded to Vincent.

I glanced at Vincent and stuck out my tongue. "More than I want to know."

Batholomew smirked and set his hands on my shoulders. He guided me over to a dirty chair in front of the desk, set me in the seat, and seated himself on the nearest corner of his desk. A small avalanche of papers fell to the floor, but he ignored them. "We seem to be off on the wrong foot," he commented.

"The wrong body," I muttered.

"Allow me to introduce myself." He slid off the desk, stepped back and bowed at me. "My name is Frederick George Arthur Phillip Bartholomew, but those whom I respect call me Bat."

I raised an eyebrow. "Bat?" I repeated.

"Yes, perhaps because I seem to have a wonderful flight of imagination," he guessed.

"Or perhaps your disposition is more batty than any fictional vampire," Vincent quipped.

Bat shot him a glare, but turned back to me. "And what's your name?"

"Liz Stokes."

"Short for Elizabeth?"

"Yeah."

"A very pretty name." Bat walked around the desk, righted his chair and seated himself. He clapped his hands together and frowned. "Well, now that we have that polite gesture out of the way let's get down to business. Judging by your answer to my earlier question can I safely assume you know nothing of what's happened regarding our mutual friend, Tim?"

"All I know is Tim was my roommate, and now he's dead and I'm somehow stuck with this walking corpse." I jerked my thumb toward Vincent, who rolled his eyes.

Bat coughed to hide a snort. "I see. That isn't much to go off of to understand your current predicament."

"And what's my current predicament?"

"That you've fallen into the thick of the world of the supernatural and are now bound to a very foolish and dangerous fellow."

Chapter 5

My face fell and my hands shook. I balled them together in my lap, but I couldn't ball my emotions together. They were all over the place. There was fear, sadness, fear, confusion, fear, curiosity, and did I mention fear?

"Come again?" I asked him.

"You have fallen into the world of vampires, ghosts, goblins, and the like," he rephrased.

"Uh-huh, and how do I get out of this world?" I wondered.

Bat leaned over the desk and the lamp cast shadows on the creases of his ancient face. "I'm afraid there's no escaping this world. Once you've dived into the rabbit hole the only way to go is forward and hope nothing snatches you from the shadows."

I leaned back and cringed. "Have you taken your medication lately?"

His eyebrows shot up and he sat back. "Now that you mention it, no." He opened a top drawer, pulled out a plastic container of pills, and popped a few into his mouth. "There. All better."

"So there's a way I can get out of this mess?"

"Oh no, there's no way in hell you can escape this mess. Or rather, you *are* in hell and there's no way out."

I numbly stood and my shaky legs tried to collapse, but I grasped the back of my chair. "I-I think I need to get back to my apartment. I have some-um, some pants to fold."

Bat smiled and shook his head. "I'm afraid that wouldn't be a wise idea. You may as well accept that your old life has vanished."

I glared at him. "Um, no? I'm not going to throw aside twenty-well, a lot of years of living because of a one-night stand with Count Creepy here." I gestured to Vincent, who was amused by my title for him.

"You mistake my meaning, Miss Stokes. You are very much mistaken in my intentions toward you. I only want the best for you and that ring you wear." He nodded at the metal band around my finger. "After all, both of you are the only possessions we have of Tim, and I'm sure he'd want his friends and-" he frowned and glanced at Vincent. "-acquaintances to care for them."

"First off, I'm nobody's possession. Second, I think this is all some horrible dream and if I ran into a wall I'd probably wake up," I countered.

Bat smiled and waved his hand at the far wall to my right. "Go right ahead, Miss Stokes, but be careful not to hit too hard. We wouldn't want you to receive a concussion for nothing."

I looked at the wall and decided maybe this wasn't a dream. "Or maybe I just need a really long nap and I can decide what to do after that," I suggested.

"I have a comfortable couch somewhere in this mess," Bat offered.

"My bed would work better, and I wouldn't want to trouble you guys." I backed up toward the entrance. "I mean, I've been enough trouble and-" My back hit something hard, and I didn't need to look around to know it was Vincent's body. My face fell and I tilted my head back to find myself staring into his dark eyes. "You're not going to let me leave, are you?"

"We can't, Miss Stokes," Bat insisted as he walked around the desk. "It's in all of our best interests that you stay here, at least for tonight."

I glared at the old man. "You think I'm so important with this ring then why don't you have this stupid thing?" I raised my ring hand, grasped the ring and gave it a hard pull. It didn't budge, and the only reward for my effort was a sore finger. I pulled again, but with the same painful result. "Anybody have a can of grease or oil?" I asked them.

Bat chuckled and walked up to me. He pointed at the ring. "That's stuck to you until you can learn to get it off."

"Learn to get it off? I'm pretty sure rings are supposed to just slip off," I shot back.

"Not this one. This one is a very unique ring."

I rolled my eyes and dropped my arms to my side. "I know, I know, forged with blood and some voodoo magic to bind us."

Bat raised an eyebrow and glanced at Vincent. "So this bag of hydrated dust has told you some things?" he guessed.

"Only that I'm stuck with him, but not for how long and how I'm supposed to get out of this mess," I replied.

Bat chuckled. "I can possibly give you answers to both those questions, but I'm afraid you're not going to like them," he told me.

I shrugged. "You just told me I'm stuck in this weird place with two weirdos after being chased by some crazy guys with a werewolf. How can this night possibly get worse?"

"It can get worse because you are going to have quite a few more nights with such, shall we call it, fun?" he answered.

My jaw jutted out and I glared at him. "Come again?"

Bat smiled and walked over to my chair. He turned it toward me and gestured to the seat. "If you would care to sit down again I will tell you what I can about that ring, our mutual friend Tim, and that ring that is stuck on your finger."

I frowned, but walked over and sat down in the chair. I folded my arms across my chest, crossed my legs, and tapped a finger on my arm. "I'm listening."

Bat walked in the space between my chair and the desk. "First off, your partner here is someone whom you shouldn't trust," he told me. Vincent frowned, but remained silent. "Secondly, that ring is the only item keeping him from killing us both."

"Then this thing's not doing a very good job because he's already tried that twice," I quipped.

Bat raised an eyebrow. "Really? Was the bond awakened?"

"As soon as you tell me what exactly this bond is I can answer that." I jerked my thumb at the silent undead. For the first time I wished he'd speak up. "He told me I was stuck with him and he'd protect me. He also said this ring would give me some sort of vampire powers."

"For once he's told the truth," Bat mused. "The ring does give you abilities beyond those of a normal human being, but only so long as you wear it."

"Right now that's not a problem."

Bat frowned and seated himself on the end of his desk. "Perhaps I am going about this the wrong way. Let me start at the beginning with Tim. He inherited the ring a few centuries ago from the original owner, the human who's blood is encased in that ring."

I blinked. "Centuries? You mean years, don't you?" I asked him.

Bat smiled and shook his head. "No, I mean centuries. The ring granted Tim a sort of immortality. So long as he wore the ring and this fool protected him, he wouldn't die."

My mouth slowly fell open and images of our lovemaking flashed through my mind. I shuddered. "Okay, that's just creepy. He didn't look a day over thirty."

"The ring froze his appearance, though I wish his mind had aged a little further," Bat mused with a playful grin on his face. He shook himself from his thoughts and pointed at the ring on my finger. "It has done the same to your appearance, though you don't know it yet, and so long as there isn't another lapse in protection then you will live a very long and eventful life."

"What if I don't want to live forever?" I countered.

"I'm afraid that is not an option. Once the bond is created only death can break it."

I stood so quickly I knocked my chair over. "So what the hell am I supposed to do for eternity? Pick up Social Security until I drain it dry?" I angrily asked them.

Bat slid off the desk and walked around the desk to his chair. "I recommend a hobby or an occupation." He paused in front of his chair and tapped a long nail against his chin. His eyes lit up with mischief. "Yes, that may work."

"What now?" I asked him, perfectly expecting more wonderful news.

"With Tim no longer with us his business will need a new owner. I think you would suit the role perfectly."

"Um, no?" I replied. Everything else I'd been dragged into that evening had been trouble.

Vincent had of the same opinion. "She isn't competent enough to manage the business," he spoke up.

Bat shrugged. "Perhaps not, but you can teach her."

Both Vincent and I jerked back in surprise. "No!" we shouted in unison.

The old man sat down in his chair and grinned at us over his entwined hands. "See? You two are getting along famously already. This should make your partnership much easier," he commented.

"Are you listening to either of us?" I asked him. "I don't know what this business was, but if it had anything to do with Tim's death I don't think I want to work in it."

"I believe it was exactly why Tim was killed, or shall we say murdered," Bat replied. I flinched. That's how the cop had phrased it. "I see I hit the hammer on the nail. What can you tell us about his death?"

I cringed and hesitantly shrugged. "Only that the cops think he was murdered."

Bat leaned back in his chair and nearly fell over. "How interesting that the police would be involved. Tim's dealings were outside their capacity as enforcers of human laws."

I'd had enough with this talk of humans, vampires and werewolves. I nervously smiled and backed up away from the desk. "You probably have a lot to think about with Tim-well, with Tim not being around." I felt a lump in my throat at that thought. "So I'll leave you two guys alone to deal with this and just be on my way." I spun around and found myself staring into Vincent's coat. I jumped back and threw up my arms. "Come on! I have no idea what you guys are talking about or what you want from me, okay? I'm just a stupid office girl who had a strange roommate. That's it! Nothing special about normal old me!"

"Tim evidently thought you were special enough to room with," Bat countered.

I spun around and glared at Bat. "Tim's dead!" I shot back. I cringed at my own words and at the hurt expression on the old man's face, but I wouldn't give up my chance to leave Crazy-ville. I sighed and my shoulders drooped. "Please just let me go. I promise I won't tell anyone about this place, or Vincent, or anything I saw tonight."

I expected some suave words to try to coax me back, but Bat sighed and gave a nod. "Very well. We will let you return to your normal life," he agreed.

I narrowed my eyes and leaned my head toward him. "You're not fooling me, are you?"

"Fooling you?" he repeated.

"Yeah, tricking me. Making me think I can get out of here and then WHAM! You drag me back kicking and screaming and convince me to stay."

Bat chuckled. "No. You are free to go, and we won't stop you from returning to your old life."

I backed up away from the desk and my eyes flickered between the pair. "All right, then. I guess I'll be going."

"It was a pleasure meeting you, Miss Stokes," Bat bid me farewell.

"The pleasure was all yours," I mumbled. I knocked my back into one of the research tables, and sheepishly grinned at him. "Um, be seeing you."

I swung around and sprinted toward the front door. There were no hurried footsteps behind me, no shouts to stop. I hit the door, flung it open, and burst out into the cool, clean night air. I took a deep breath of the city air and choked on some exhaust. Yep, I was free.

Chapter 6

Unfortunately, I was also totally lost. I had no idea where I was, and with all the creepiness of that night I even doubted *when* I was. The stars would have been useful if I knew how to read them, but since I didn't know the Ursa Major from a C Minor I took off in a random direction. There were only four cardinal directions to go. How wrong could I be? Apparently very wrong.

I managed to get out of the forest of dilapidated factories and into one of the less luxurious parts of town. There were abandoned cars without tires, or even rims, and every window in the tall apartment buildings was broken. The roads were potholes with short strips of broken concrete. Walls that weren't spray-painted with graffiti were- wait, there were no walls that didn't have graffiti. Shop doors were ajar because thieves had already stolen everything of value, and on the stoops of several apartment buildings sat the thieves themselves. They leered at me, and I shakily smiled back and hurried on. Far off I heard sirens and gunshots. The sirens faded into the distance, but the gunshots got closer. The whole place made my crummy street look like Malibu-Fort Knox.

Some of the stoop stooges decided I looked a little lost, which I was, and wanted to offer their help, which I didn't want. A particularly bad crowd, they had tattoos, buzz-cuts, and torn, blood-stained clothing, followed me off the steps of their wrecked apartment building. I nervously glanced back, and they hollered and hooted at me. It would take more than a few catcalls to flatter me, it would take them taking a bath.

I hurried my steps along the filthy street with no end to the ruin in sight. The men picked up their speed, and my instincts took over. They told me to run. I shot off down the street and the men gave chase, calling for me to stop. They whispered sweet promises of rape if I stopped, and promises of rape-murder if I didn't. None of those choices sounded good to me, but they were much faster than me. I thought to lose them in the maze of alleys that were pocketed between the apartment buildings, so I shot into the first one I came to. Bad idea. I ran a dozen yards down the alley before I realized a ten-foot tall brick wall stood in my path. It was a dead end, and the guys behind me meant to make that a literal description.

I skidded to a stop at the end of the alley and swung around to find the silhouette of the gang members standing in the opening to the alley. Their brass knuckles shined in the weak starlight, and their chuckles froze my blood. One of them, the leader, stepped forward. He was a particularly impressive specimen of his kind with yellowed, chipped teeth, a bald head that was marked with battle scars, and clothes that just screamed *run, ladies!*

He looked me over with a lecherous grin. "You look a little lost, lamb," he remarked. His cohorts snickered and tussled each other for the line behind their leader. He had first grabs on me. "Want us to help ya out?"

"N-no, I'm fine. Just going for a night stroll," I replied.

"The night can be pretty dangerous," the man commented. He took a few steps toward me and towered over my small, quivering frame. "Why don't ya let us help ya? We don't ask much."

"I don't have any money on me, so I guess I'll just have to find my own way." I tried to slip past him, but he grabbed my shoulder and pulled my back against his large, stinking chest. His hands wrapped around me and pinned me to him.

He leaned down and his breath smelled like the bottom of a public toilet. "Not so fast, girlie. Let's have some fun first, and then we'll let ya go. Maybe." One of his hands reached up and cupped my breast.

I squirmed and pulled, but I couldn't free myself. "No! Please don't!" I cried out.

"The night is too dangerous for you," a smooth voice spoke up. The men and I glanced at the front of the alley and saw-actually, we didn't see anyone there.

I took advantage of the guy's distraction by slipping down out of his grasp and jumping away from him. Unfortunately, that way was toward the brick wall. "You'd better do what the creepy voice said or it'll, um, bore you to death," I warned them.

The leader blinked, and a grin replaced his confused expression. He let out a great, bellowing laugh, and his minions hesitantly joined in. The man sneered and glanced around at the shadows. "Whoever ya are get out here and face us! Or are ya too scared to mess with my gang?" he challenged.

"Not too scared," the voice replied. I screamed when a form melted out of the shadows of the building right beside me. That fright nearly gave me the energy to scale the brick wall behind me, but I didn't try when I realized it was Vincent at my side. "Too indifferent," he added.

"Don't scare me like that!" I scolded him as I clutched onto my chest. My heart was playing drums for a heavy metal band, and it was on a solo part.

Fortunately, the leader was also frightened by Vincent's appearance and he stumbled back a few yards. "What the hell? Where did you come from?"

"Your nightmares," Vincent replied before he dove at the gang leader. Vincent latched onto the man's neck, and the leader changed from a bold, giant brute to a scared little girl in one high-pitched scream. His scream was cut off when he was struck with the lethargy of the vampire bite. The men behind him made a chorus of tenors as they turned tail and ran. Vincent flung the man backward and the gang leader sailed past me and hit face-first into the brick wall. The vampire shot off after the retreating gang members and I was glad when they all rounded the corners and I could only hear their terror rather than see what Vincent was doing to them.

I also didn't want to stick around to see what plans Vincent had for me. I swung around and saw my way out in the form of the would-be rapist. The man was aware enough to raise himself on his hands and knees, and that gave me just the boost I needed. I ran at him, jumped onto his solid back, and used him as a springboard to grasp the top of the brick wall. The gang leader crumbled beneath my shoes, but I had my hold and pulled myself over. I dropped down the other side and high-tailed it down the other side of the alley. I didn't get far before a moving shadow swooped out of the unmoving shadows and stood in my way.

"I'm not going back with you," I refused.

Vincent's voice was flat-line and bored. "That isn't why I followed you," he replied.

I raised an eyebrow and narrowed my eyes. "Then why did you follow me? Feeling a bit peckish?"

"I'm fond of my existence, and my existence is bound to yours. If you die, I die," he reminded me.

"So you were just saving your own neck by biting theirs?" I quipped.

"Exactly. I was also thirsty. You drained me of most of my energy."

"You mean with that glowy light thing?" I guessed, and he nodded. "What was that, anyway?"

"Your body reacted to danger and your wound by stealing my life-force to rejuvenate your own."

I snorted. "I like to think of it as permanent borrowing."

"I don't care."

I frowned and crossed my arms. "Obviously, but mind getting out of my way so we can go our separate ways?"

"Without a guide you will destroy us both," he argued.

"Are you trying to tell me that I can't take care of myself?" I asked him.

"Wouldn't think of it," he blandly replied.

"Good, because otherwise I'd have to kill you, or destroy you, or whatever I need to do to make you into something a vacuum can take care of."

"That would kill you," he pointed out.

I waved away his comment. "Details, details, now are you going to be my guide or do I have to go off and practice my damsel-in-distress routine again?" Vincent's mouth straightened into a perfect line, and before I could stop him he'd lifted me in his arms and sped out of the alley and down the street.

The wind whipped past us, and my hair whipped me. "I can walk!" I protested as I pulled my hair out of my mouth and eyes.

"Your ability is not in question, it is the speed that is up for debate," he replied.

"My speed is just fine for a human!"

"Your speed is pathetic for what you have become."

I rolled my eyes. "Don't give me the same b.s. that Bat was saying, or I'll slug you with a cross."

40

"That is mere fiction," he retorted.

"Baseball bat smothered in garlic?" I suggested.

"That is fact."

"Then I'll beat you with a bat if you don't let me-"

"We're there." Vincent jerked to a stop and unceremoniously dropped me to the hard ground. I yelped and glared up at him as I rubbed my wounded posterior.

"Could you give a warning before you put on the brakes? Something like a light on your nose blinking?" I requested.

"Look around."

I growled, but my eyes heeded his command and glanced around us. That's when I realized we stood in front of my apartment building. We'd covered a dozen miles in one bantering session. "Wow," I murmured in awe.

"If you can take care of yourself than surely you have no more need of me. Goodnight." He whipped away down the street, but managed to whip my hair into my eyes one last time.

I pulled the loose strands aside and growled. "That vampire is more than a pain in the neck," I grumbled. I stood and hurried inside to escape the dark and the stupid creatures it held. My apartment was safely reached, but then I realized I'd lost my key during all the 'fun' of the evening.

Chapter 7

Unfortunately, that was just fine because my door was ajar. Well, it was still a door, but an open one, and glancing inside I could see someone had redecorated. Every piece of furniture was upside down and the stuffings ripped out of it. Tables lay on their sides and every piece of china was broken. I tripped inside and gaped at the mess. "What the hell-?" I whispered.

I stumbled over the ruins of my belongings and my life. Nothing was untouched by the destructive hands. I reached the television and my foot crunched down on glass. I glanced down and saw I'd stepped on a wooden frame. It's glass covering was broken, and when I picked it up I saw the image was torn. It was a picture of Tim and me smiling. We'd convinced Vincent to take it a few years ago because he didn't want to be in it. I imagined a lack of reflection had something to do with that.

Tears sprang into my eyes and I stumbled back to sit on the overturned front end of the couch. I wasn't sure who'd done this, but I had a feeling it was those two cops. My free hand balled into a fist and I smashed it against the bottom of the couch. I regretted it when the hard wood frame beat out my soft, squishy hand, and to make matters worse I was still mad. I took the picture out of the frame and tucked it safely inside my jeans pocket.

As for the rest of the place, I opted to leave it until I was sure what I wanted to do. Calling the cops would probably bring Tweedle Dee and Tweedle Dum, and they'd make the same mess of me as they had of my apartment. I did right the living room chair and an end table to make the crime scene a little more homey. I'd just plopped down for a really long nap when my stomach growled. I hadn't had anything to eat in a few terrifying, adrenaline-draining hours.

At my stomach's bidding I walked over to the kitchen and opened the fridge. I glanced inside and my stomach churned at the various states of decomposing vegetables and spoiled milk. Unfortunately, or fortunately, I wasn't peckish for any of that and shut the door. A scouring of the cupboards succeeded in making me hungrier, but I still didn't find something I wanted to munch on.

I growled and turned away from the cupboards just in time to see a shadow flash by the fire escape that stood outside one of the living room windows. My eyes widened and I waited for something epic and terrifying to happen. A minute ticked by and I decided waiting for something epic was boring, so I slunk over to the side of the window. I peeked my head around the edge of the frame.

A large shadow loomed on the metal grate, and our eyes met. My bright blue ones widened and its yellow-orange ones narrowed. The thing jumped at the window, and I ducked as shards of glass rained down on me. I heard a growl and whipped my head up. Standing in my living room was another one of those wolf beasts, and this time I was close enough to catch a whiff of its breath. It smelled like it'd just ate somebody for dinner, and I was the dessert. The creature's orange eyes gazed at me and I scrambled back on my hands and rear. The thing quickly followed and reached out one of its clawed hands to grab me.

My savior shadow swooped in through the broken window and knocked into it. The werewolf slammed to the floor, and Vincent jumped off its back and deftly landed beside me. He grabbed my shirt collar and yanked me to my feet. "You are doing an admirable job of staying alive," he quipped.

I scowled at him and poked a finger into his chest. "Don't you dare tell me I can't-ah!" I yelped when Vincent grabbed my head and shoved it down to avoid a wide swipe of the creature's claws.

"Your survival skills are impressive," he quipped. I tried to reply, but he shoved me out of the way as the werewolf lunged at us, and he himself dove to the left. The beast hit air and dug his claws into the carpet. I never liked that color, anyway.

I rolled over the floor and hit the side of my chair. I was quick to recover, and glared at Vincent who stood across the room. "All right, so I can't take care of myself! You want me to give you a bone for being right?" The werewolf swung its head around and snarled at me. I held up my hands in front of me and nervously smiled. "No, doggy. I don't really have any bones."

The beast leapt at me, and I screamed and rolled out of the way. Its claws were buried into the side of my chair and tore most of its stuffing from the arm. I tried to stand, but it grabbed my foot and yanked me toward it. My hands clawed at the carpet, but the werewolf dragged me back. Vincent flew by me and knocked into the werewolf. He slammed the beast into the wall, and I heard the screams of my frightened neighbors on the other side. I could just imagine them dialing 911, and that meant we only had a few hours until the police arrived, too late and undermanned.

Apparently Vincent thought the same because he jumped back from the wolf thing and picked up a large shard of glass from the window. The beast pulled itself from its crater in the wall and roared. It was reckless with anger and lunged at Vincent without seeing what he was holding. Unfortunately, I saw everything, including when Vincent coolly sliced the air with the shard of glass. The sharp, homemade blade cut clear through the beast's head, and its blood splattered the entire room. I wasn't spared from the blood shower, and my filthy clothes were further filthed by the disgusting red dye of life fluid.

Vincent tossed aside the glass and strode over to me. He knelt in front of me and looked me over. "Are you all right?" he asked me.

I replied in the only sensible way a girl could. I fainted.

Chapter 8

I don't know how long I was out, but when I woke up I wasn't in Kansas, anymore, or at least not in my apartment. My eyes fluttered open and I found myself staring at a white ceiling with a simple light fixture. I turned my head and noticed it was a whole room of blandness, but I lay on a couch that looked like one of those ones used for mental patients. For one wild moment I considered the whole thing a dream and me a psycho ward patient, but Bat sat close by in a chair. Behind him sat a dresser and to the right of that was the door out of the room. The couch I lay on sat against the opposite wall, and on the same wall but in the opposite corner stood a refrigerator.

I wasn't sure whether to be glad or depressed to see him. I'd been saved from the nightmare of my apartment and shoved back into the weirdness that was him. I sat up and winced when my head complained of the movement. That knock against the chair gave me a delicious ostrich egg complete with scrambled brains.

"Is there a doctor in the house?" I muttered.

Bat chuckled. "I have several PhD's, but none that quickens the healing process," he replied. "How are you feeling?"

I rubbed my sore head. "Like I was run over by the Werewolf Express."

"Yes, an experience with a werewolf leaves one with a few knocks and bruises," he agreed.

"And stains," I added as I looked down at myself. My clothes were speckled by the werewolf's blood. "Any way I can get a spare shirt?"

Bat stood and walked over to the dresser. He opened a drawer and revealed a long line of spare white shirts like what he wore. "If you don't mind wearing my size," he teased.

"I think I can handle it." He tossed me a shirt and turned to give me some privacy. I slipped off the blood rag and slipped on the clean shirt.

"What do you think about my proposition now?" Bat spoke up.

I tossed my shirt off the end of the couch and looked back to him. "What proposition?" I asked him.

"About changing your life. Vincent and I swore we would let you return to your old life, but your enemies will not be as lenient."

"That would have been nice to know before I nearly got myself killed," I snapped. I paused and furrowed my brow. "Wait a sec. My enemies? I didn't do anything to them, unless they hate me for existing."

"Existing with Tim's ring," he added. "That ring grants immortality to any mortal, and they prefer to keep their mortals mortal. It makes humans easier to handle."

"Who is they, anyway? I feel like we're talking about Voldemort here."

"The Syndicate," Bat replied.

"The Syndicate?" I'd entered a really bad horror novel.

"A Sanguine Syndicate, to be exact, for there are many in the world, though none as dangerous as the one in this city. We often shorten it to ASS in conversations." I choked on my spittle and he smiled. "It's a pleasure to hear you laugh at my jokes. I was afraid Tim had been replaced with a person who held the same sense of humor as Vincent."

I scowled at him. "I'm nothing like that-that-"

"-vampire?" he finished for me.

"Among other things," I agreed.

"From what little I have learned of your temperament I would say you two are of opposite dispositions."

"Huh?"

"Your personalities don't get along."

"Um, thanks. I think." I swung my legs over the side of the couch and sighed. "So what do I do now that my apartment's been redecorated with red paint and couch stuffing?"

"You continue living, but as a different person."

"After being the same person for-well, for a lot of years that's not easy to do," I pointed out.

"Nonsense. No one remains the same person they were when they were born, or even who they were a year ago. Everyone changes, but how many people can say they have the opportunity to completely change their lives?"

"Serial killers with alternate lives and people suffering from a split-personality disorder," I quipped.

"Those people, and you," he replied. "You have an incredibly unique chance to change who you are, and possibly find the person you were always meant to be."

"I'm pretty sure I was meant to be a secretary. It isn't what my degree in art history prepared me for, but I'm not complaining," I returned.

"And you've never wanted to be someone else?"

"Does that someone else happen to have a dangerous job that involves working with a deadly vampire and running from even deadlier werewolves and guys with guns?"

"Yes."

"Then no, I haven't wanted to be someone else." I glanced around the room occupied only by the two of us. "Speaking of someone else, where's tall, dark and gruesome?"

"He's currently hiding your tracks and confusing other pets of the Syndicate with false trails," Bat told me.

"Helpful of him," I commented.

"He prefers to stay alive. So would I," Bat replied.

"I'll third that wish, but 'my enemies' don't seem to want that to happen."

"You would be much safer with Vincent," he hinted.

"Uh-huh, living the life that was meant for me?" I quipped.

"Yes, actually. That is, unless you wish to return to your apartment," he slyly commented.

"You know you're evil, right?"

"I have been called many things, but I prefer the term eccentric."

"I prefer to have my life back, but I don't think either of us are getting what we want.".

"Perhaps you don't know what you want, and a breath of fresh life would be just the trick."

"You're not going to give up 'helping' me find my new life, are you?" I asked him.

Bat smiled and shook his head. "I'm afraid not."

I sighed and my shoulders slumped. "Since I'm kind of tired of running around and almost getting killed, how about we make a deal? I'll try out this life like I would a used pair of pants. If I find it doesn't fit then I'm returning the life and hopefully this ring to you just as soon as I figure out how Tim got it off."

"Your life was never mine to begin with," he corrected me.

"Well, I'll give them to you, anyway. Deal?" I held out my hand, and he took it in a strong handshake. I would never have guessed he had that much energy.

"Deal, but how long will you try this experiment?" he asked me.

"If I survive long enough I'll try it out for a few weeks," I suggested.

Bat grinned and rubbed his hands together. "Excellent. Now all we need do is wait for that undead fool to return and we will make plans for the near future."

"You know, I get the feeling you two don't like each other. Mind telling me the back-story so I'm not totally lost?" I requested.

He chuckled. "A woman and gossip are never far apart, but I'm afraid the tale would be too long."

I gestured around the room and crossed my arms over my chest. "I have time."

Bat opened his mouth, then paused and glanced over his shoulder at the closed door. "It seems you don't have time. Vincent has returned." A few moments later the door opened and Vincent slipped inside. I hadn't heard a thing.

"How'd you do that?" I asked Bat.

"Practice, and the stench of his clothing. He bathes once every century." I'd been so panicked every time I'd been in Vincent's arms, and the wind had blown by us so fast, that I hadn't noticed the stench. Now that it was pointed out I took in the full glory of the smell. It was a mixture of skunk and sulfur with a dash of cow fart to add some flavor.

I gagged and slapped my hand over my nose. "If we're going to be stuck together you're going to have to bath," I honked through my hand. Vincent took my suggestion and filed it under his I-don't-give-a-shit expression.

"It's nearly sunrise," Bat informed us. "You'll have to hurry if you're going to show the lovely Miss Stokes her new home."

Vincent raised an eyebrow and glanced over to me. I shrugged. "I don't have anything better to do," I pointed out.

"Then it's agreed. You two shall begin your new life together tonight," Bat spoke up. He turned to Vincent. "Which location will you choose?"

"Park Place," he replied.

I thought it sounded good enough, it was one of the high-end Monopoly places, but Bat frowned. "Isn't there a better location?" he wondered.

"Yes."

Bat waited for an explanation, but decided eternity was too long. He gave Vincent one last scowl before he turned to me with a smile. "I'm sure you will make yourself comfortable there once you have had time to settle in." Something in his voice didn't bring me comfort, but I had a few other things on my mind.

"Before I dive headfirst into the deep end of the Weirds-ville pool is there anything else I need to know about this ring thing? You two said I'd be getting some of Vincent's powers, but do I need to sleep in a coffin all day?" I asked the pair.

"No, but your diet has changed," Bat replied.

I narrowed my eyes. "How?"

"Let me put it this way: your sole sustenance is now hemoglobin."

"Huh?"

"Blood, Miss Stokes. You now survive on blood."

The blood drained from my face. "What?"

"It's just a minor side effect to the ring. You can still eat human food, but it won't satisfy your hunger," Bat explained to me.

51

I threw up my arms and my voice bounced off the walls of the white room. "Just a minor side effect?" I yelled. "You just told me I have to kill people to survive!"

"I said no such thing. I merely said you needed blood to survive," he corrected me.

"Same thing!"

"Not at all. You can take blood from a human without killing them, or you can take a donation from the local blood bank."

"Are you mad?" I screamed.

"That is a matter of opinion, but I have been called that."

"I am not going to be drinking blood to survive! That's just-" I froze when Bat whipped out a long, sharp knife from inside his shirt. The blade glistened in the weak light above us, but it reflected the gleam in his eyes. I scrambled back against the wall behind the couch. "W-what are you doing with that?" I stuttered.

"Proving a point." He pulled back his sleeve and drew the blade across skin on the underside of his arm. A thin line of blood rose up and poured over the sides of his limb. I cringed when he held his arm out to me. "Doesn't that look yummy?" he teased.

"You're really sick, you know that?" I asked him.

"Yes, but aren't you a little hungry?" My stomach answered for us both when it broke out in a loud roar. Bat chuckled. "That proves that point. Wouldn't you want a sip? Just a tiny bit to satisfy that gnawing inside of you?"

The scent of the blood hit my nose and my nostrils flared. The liquid *did* smell good, but this wasn't a raspberry-strawberry smoothy. He offered me blood. I wanted to close my eyes, but my stomach growled again and my gaze was drawn to the clear, thick liquid. Just one little sip wouldn't hurt anybody. He'd already cut himself so it'd be a waste to let-what the hell was I thinking?

"Take it. It's not often you find a willing victim," Vincent spoke up.

I cast a quick glare at him, but my gaze invariably returned to the blood. Bat scooted closer and held out his arm. "It's getting cold," he commented.

I hated to admit it to myself, but that stuff looked really tempting. That shining blood glistened and called to me. My tongue flicked out and licked my lips, but it caught on my canines. My incredibly long canines. I clapped a hand over my mouth and my eyes widened when I felt the length of those sharp teeth. That wasn't right, but they were useful.

Vincent sneered at me. "Don't waste any more blood on her," he told Bat. "She's too stupid to-" I surprised him, and myself, by lunging forward and clamping my new teeth down on Bat's wound. He didn't even flinch when my fangs sank deep into his skin, and I drained a few quarts before he gently but firmly pulled me away.

I coughed on the last sip of blood and raised a shaking hand to my lips. My teeth slipped back to their normal length, and all the remained of my feasting was a smudge of blood on one side of my lips. The hunger inside of me disappeared and my body slid into the lethargy of food satisfaction.

Bat's face was almost as pale as Vincent's own and his breathing was a little ragged, but he had a kind smile on his lips. "I think that might be enough for now," he told me. I stared at him dumbly, unsure what just happened. Bat took a handkerchief out from his pocket and offered it to me. "You have relatively clean dinner manners," he teased.

I took the handkerchief in my shaking hand and quickly wiped the evidence off me. I felt both sick and satisfied.

Vincent stepped forward. "If this pathetic display is done then we need to leave," he reminded us.

I was too shaken to move, and Bat glared at him. "It's a useful lesson, one you should have given yourself if you were useful," he shot back.

Vincent didn't reply, but strode over and lifted me into his arms. I yelped in surprise and clung to him. "Don't you ever ask?" I yelled at him.

"No."

"Now you two children behave living in an apartment all by yourself," Bat playfully scolded.

I was mid-gag when Vincent sped us out of there and off to my new home.

Chapter 9

Park Place wasn't the expensive Monopoly real estate I was expecting. Instead it was a neighborhood slightly more upscale than slums, and with the same broken windows and broken down buildings I'd seen on my escape from the factories. You know, the lovely place where I'd almost been raped. Vincent stopped our land-speed record in front of a particularly dilapidated apartment building. He set me down and strode up the stoop, leaving me to follow after him.

The foyer was an artistic representation of wreck and ruin. The wood floor boards were broken and scattered everywhere, there were cobwebs in places I didn't know cobwebs could hang, and the rats looked like they'd formed a biker's gang to poop and pee on every inch of walk space. It was just lovely.

I was still numb from my recent blood transfusion, but not numb enough to be blind nor lacking in sarcasm. "Um, not to be ungrateful or anything, but isn't there a-I don't know, a less diseased place to live?" I asked him.

He didn't reply as he strode up the flight of stairs that looked made of splinters rather than boards. I carefully hurried after him, afraid my foot would fall through a step and he'd abandon me to fend off the rats alone and unarmed. We climbed the Stairs of Doom until we hit the fifth floor out of seven. I didn't think this place was very lucky as Vincent led me down the hall past broken and missing doors. He stopped at the single sturdy-looking door, opened it, and stepped into the apartment. I peeked my head in.

It was a hell of a lot better than the rest of the apartment building, but that was like comparing a trailer park before and after a tornado went through. The floors were new vinyl that hadn't been cleaned since installation, the walls were painted to hide the water stains, and the filthy windows would have looked out on an alley if you could see out of them. Even in the middle of the day this place wouldn't get much sunlight. "Cozy," I quipped as I slipped inside.

The bare pieces of furniture consisted of a couch that saw better days a few decades ago, a long, rectangular box in front of it with cup stains on the lid, and a few broken wooden chairs. The kitchen on the right was bare of everything except cobwebs and the two rooms to the left were the bedroom and bath. The bath was the epitome of bachelor pad filth with stains of questionable age and origin, and the bedroom had a bed covered with dusty sheets.

Vincent strode across the room to the windows opposite the entrance and brushed aside what I guessed was a curtain and not torn cloths. He piqued my curiosity when he glanced outside, and I sidled up next to him. "Any werewolves out there?" I half joked.

"We weren't followed," he assured me. He let down the rags-formerly-known-as-curtains and turned his attention to the box. He brushed past me and over to the stained wood. "I will rest for the day. Don't leave the apartment."

I followed him and watched as he pushed aside the lid to reveal the inside. No padding, no pillow, not even a teddy bear with fangs. "What if the place catches fire?" I asked him.

"Haul me to the basement. It's fireproof," he replied as he slid into the box.

"But I don't know where the basement is, and you told me not to leave the apartment," I pointed out.

Vincent paused in an upright position and his lips pursed tightly together. "Don't leave the apartment building," he appended. Then he lay down and shut the lid over himself.

That gave me more roaming room, but I had a problem in the apartment. Actually, the problem was with the apartment itself. I wasn't the cleanest person on earth, or even in my old apartment, but this place wasn't habitable to anyone except a bachelor and the undead. It looked like I would be cleaning my apartment this weekend after all, it just happened to be in a different neighborhood with a different roommate.

I rummaged through the bedroom closet and one out in the living room, and managed to scrounge up a vacuum that was a few years old and looked like it'd never been used. I also commandeered the rags-formerly-known-as-curtain and turned them into dust rags. The tap had clean-looking water, and there was some dish soap beneath the sink. Armed with all the weapons of war, I waged battle on the messiness.

Everything went fine until I turned on the vacuum. I jumped and my head tapped the ceiling when the lid to the coffin flung open and Vincent sat up.

"What the hell are you doing?" he growled at me.

I hugged the vacuum neck against my chest in the hopes it would keep the dirty vampire at bay. "I thought vampires were supposed to sleep like the dead during the day," I replied.

"If that were true my species would have been vanquished long ago," he pointed out.

"Good point, but I'm not going to stop vacuuming just because you're a light sleeper," I argued. "Besides, it's not like it's going to kill you to lose some sleep."

"Decreased energy helps our enemies," he countered.

"If you and Tim hadn't built up so many enemies then you wouldn't need all that energy," I argued.

"It was unavoidable."

"It was bad diplomacy."

Vincent growled through gritted teeth, lay down, and slammed the box lid back down. I resumed my vacuuming, but was again rudely interrupted when he tossed aside the lid and stood. "Do you mean to vex me the entire day?" he wondered.

"It'll take that long to get this place cleaned up," I quipped.

Vincent stepped out of his bed and tried to grab the vacuum from my hands. He ended up dragging me along with it. "Give that to me," he ordered.

"Over your dead body," I returned. Vincent raised the vacuum over his head, but I clung onto the neck and went up with it. I dangled in the air and my face was even with his. "How about we call a truce?" I suggested.

"No."

"There's that bad diplomacy habit again. You need to learn to give a little."

"I gave you my energy."

"That was unwilling. I'm talking about a deal."

"My demand is the vacuum."

"No deal."

"Then we are at an impasse."

"No, we are at a dingy apartment building in a slightly less dingy apartment. I'm trying to remedy that, but you're not helping."

"It doesn't need remedying."

"I thought you'd say something like that."

"Let go of the vacuum."

"How about I not vacuum until sunset? Deal?"

Vincent's eyes narrowed and he perused my face with a careful glance. "On what do you swear?"

"An American flag?" I offered. The thin lines of his lips grew thinner, and I rolled my eyes. "Fine, fine, I swear on-um, on my life?" I paused and furrowed my face. "Which I guess is kind of your life since we're bonded. This is kind of like marriage, but without the fun honeymoon. Or maybe this is the fun honeymoon-"

"I will accept that." He set the vacuum down on the floor and me with it.

"All right, I guess I'll just set this back in the closet and you can get back to sleep," I replied. I expected him to climb back into his box, but after I put the vacuum in the closet and turned around I found he still stood there. "Need a bedtime story?" I wondered.

"Have you felt different?" he asked me.

"Sure, every time I walk into a black or Asian neighborhood," I replied.

If he could have killed me he would have done it right then. "Within the last hour," he amended his statement.

"Nope. Kind of tired, but nothing weird." I expected him to ask some more questions. That was my first mistake. Vincent slipped over to his bed and sat back in the box. "Wait a sec, why were you wanting to know?" I asked him. My second mistake was again thinking he was going to reply. He lay down and shut the lid over himself. I scowled and stomped over to the coffee table bed. I tried to dramatically tear off the lid, but all I got for my trouble were some dramatically deep cuts from the unfinished, splinter-filled wood. The throbbing in my fingers wouldn't deter me, so I knocked on the lid. "Why were you asking me that

59

question?" I called to him. No answer. I knocked again and still nothing happened, but I noticed the box had a nice ring to it.

That gave me an idea. I wasn't very musically inclined, but I knew the Lone Ranger theme song. It played well on the lid with my fingers as the drum sticks until it was flung aside and I came face-to-face with a very irritated Vincent. "Go away," he demanded.

"Not until you tell me why you were asking that question," I insisted.

"Merely to find out if you had come into your abilities," he replied.

"What abilities?"

"The vampiric ones given through the ring."

"Oh, right. Do those just pop out of nowhere or do they come on gradually?"

"Yes."

"I hate you."

"I don't care."

"Is there a manual for these abilities when they do pop up?"

"No."

"Not even an Idiot's Guide?"

"As much as that would suit you, no."

"You're an ass."

"I don't care."

"And not very talkative."

"I don't care."

I threw up my hands. "Come on! There's got to be some way you can help me with these abilities! Can you even tell me what I'm going to get?"

"Flight."

My eyes widened and my mouth split open in a excited smile. "Seriously?"

"No."

I don't know what made me snap. Actually, that's a lie. Vincent made me do it. It was all his fault my hand shot out and smacked him across the face. He didn't see it coming, and to be honest neither did I, but there was the red mark on his pale cheek. There was also the angry glint in his eyes, and I nervously backed up with my hands out in front of me to defend against the indefensible. "I'm so, so sorry about that. I don't usually hit people, but I guess you're not a person," I defended myself. Vincent slowly climbed out of his box and stalked toward me. I stumbled back into the wall beside the apartment door. "Y-you can't kill me, remember? The ring binding us and all that."

Vincent reached me and his hand whipped out. He grabbed my throat and lifted me off the floor. My feet flailed in the air and my hands grasped his to try to pull him off. Didn't work, but at least I tried. He stuck his face close to mine, and one whiff of his breath made me dizzy. "Never strike me in anger," he commanded.

I hated to be ordered about, especially by an undead ass. "Then stop being such an ass and answer my questions!" I snapped back. "It's not like I asked for this! I wish Tim was here so you could bite his head off with your orders, but he's not! We're stuck here together and we may as well at least get along until I figure out a way of getting this damn ring off my finger!" Vincent pursed his lips together, but he let go of me and I dropped to the ground like a bag of potatoes. I stood and rubbed my sore neck while I glared at him. "Does this mean you're going to help me with these abilities I'm supposed to get?" I asked him.

"Yes." I breathed a sigh of relief until it caught in my throat at his next words. "But I am not an easy teacher." He was one teacher I didn't think I could live through.

"I appreciate the offer, but I'm probably only going to need a few pointers," I hurriedly told him. "You know, just tell me how to, um, what am I supposed to be able to do again? And be serious this time."

"Your speed has been improved," he replied.

I furrowed my brow and gave him a disbelieving side-glance. "I said be serious."

"If your speed hadn't improved you would not have been able to hit me," he pointed out.

I raised an eyebrow. "What would you have done if I hadn't been able to hit you?"

"Caught your hand and broken it."

"That's a little extreme."

"But effective."

"You have a twisted way of thinking," I commented. Vincent suddenly turned back to the box and strode toward it. "Hey, wait! You said you'd help me with this stuff! What am I supposed to do with all this speed? How do I control it?" I lunged at him to stop him, and I overestimated my new ability. I flew across the room and would have smacked into him if he hadn't stepped to the side. I sailed by him and landed in a tangled mess of my own limbs on the couch on the other side of the box. The whole world was upside down, or I was, and I watched the upside down Vincent walk up to me. There was an evil grin on his face. "You think this is funny, don't you?" I asked him.

"Hilarious," he replied in a dead-pan voice.

I righted myself and glared at him. "You could have caught me," I scolded him.

"Yes, I could have."

"You don't regret not catching me at all, do you?"

"No."

"I hate you."

"You have already said that."

"Yeah, and you keep reminding me why I hate you."

"Your focus is very poor."

"I'm pretty focused on trying not to kill you right now," I quipped.

"Do you wish for me to train you or not?" he countered.

"I don't know, you're doing such a bang up job already," I replied as I rubbed my twisted limbs.

"You lack focus for training. Tim was much the same way."

My ears and head perked up at his comment. "So he wasn't very good when he started out?"

"He had natural talent that you completely lack," Vincent told me.

My face drooped along with my shoulders. "Thanks," I grumbled.

"Do not mention it."

"I won't, but could we start this training and see how well I actually do? Flying across the room doesn't really count as a start, though smacking you is a great one," I quipped.

"We will start when the sun sets. During the day my powers are weaker than yours, and if you were to create trouble I wouldn't be able to stop you," he replied.

I raised an eyebrow. "What kind of trouble can a little bit of speed get us into?"

He nodded behind me. "Look behind you."

I glanced over my shoulder and saw the dirty windows. My face paled when I realized the only thing that had kept me from practicing my aviation skills had been the couch. "Oh," was my reply.

"With the sun in the sky I couldn't have saved you," he added.

"Um, maybe we will wait until night."

Chapter 10

Vincent went back to bed and I went back to cleaning work, but in a quieter way. The place was scrubbed and dusted, and when he crawled out of the box after sunset he was amazed at the drastic change, or that's what I hoped for. He actually just stared around the place for all of three seconds and strode over to the door. "We have someone we need to meet," he told me.

That made me doubly disappointed. I waited all day for the chance to learn and test my abilities. "But you haven't taught me anything," I protested.

"You will learn on the way."

The only thing I learned was he was an ass, but that was something I already knew. Vincent led me from the decrepit apartment building and into the alley beside the structure. It was cleaner than the apartment building, and with fewer rats. I followed him to a pile of boxes beside a rotting wooden fence that divided the alley in half. Vincent knelt down and pushed aside the boxes to reveal a manhole. He pulled the cover off and slipped inside. I expected to hear his feet splash down in polluted water, but there was just the clack of his heels.

"Quit wasting time," he ordered me.

His voice echoed down a long metallic pipe, and I cringed. "I'm not going down there," I refused.

Vincent burst from the hole and grabbed my leg. He whipped my foot out from under me and dragged me, kicking and screaming, into the depths of a clean sewer pipe. Wait, a clean sewer pipe? I was thoroughly confused about the wide, dry culvert in which we stood. It led off in two directions, and there wasn't any light to see by. I screamed when I was swooped into someone's arms. "God damn it, Vincent, knock it off!"

"That isn't me." I froze and glanced up into the darkness where the person's head should be. Thanks to a faint, unearthly glow from the thing's eyes, I could see it had a head. Unfortunately, looking up at those eyes was like looking into the pits of Hell, and me without a roasting stick and marshmallows. The flesh was rotten and fell off in patches, and the thing's suit was ragged and also falling off in patches.

"Vincent?" I squeaked.

"Yes?" his voice came from behind the creature.

"What is this?"

"A zombie," he replied.

"We prefer the term living-challenged, but zombie will do," the creature spoke in a voice so cultured I had a craving for tea.

"Vincent!" I yelped.

"Yes?"

"The thing talks!"

"I am not a thing. My name is Officer Edward Romero of the Parasquad," the creature corrected me.

I tried to manage the panic rising inside of me and grinned nervously at the, um, officer. "Oh, he he, sorry. Mind putting me down-er, Officer Romero?" I pleaded.

"Certainly, but not until one of you tells me what you're doing down here," Officer Romero insisted.

"Vincent, what are we doing down here?" I asked my guide.

"Merely traveling to the Boo Bar," he replied.

My mouth incredulously dropped open. "Boo Bar?" I repeated. I yelped when Officer Romero set me down on my feet. I stumbled back and another pair of hands settled on my shoulders. They were Vincent's thin, strong ones.

"She new here?" the officer asked Vincent.

"Very new."

"You told her the rules yet?"

I heard Vincent scoff behind me. "I am not her keeper."

I frowned at him. "Technically, you are," I pointed out.

"Then you should tell her the rules," Officer Romero insisted.

"I intend to at a later date."

"Liar," I bit back. He squeezed my shoulders as a warning.

"It seems Vincent won't tell you, so I'll bring you up to speed. Don't kill, murder, bump off, destroy, or poof anyone out of existence," the officer warned me.

"Poof someone out of existence?" I repeated.

"It's for the witches. They're always trying to get around the rules, so we designated a phrase specifically for them," he explained.

I blinked. "Witches?"

Officer Romero's bright eyes held a worried look as he glanced at Vincent. "You sure you should take her to the Boo Bar? She's a little green," he pointed out.

"She will manage," Vincent assured him.

"I-I don't think I will. This is getting a little complicated," I piped up. Vincent didn't give me any further chance to argue when he swept me up into his arms. "I can still walk!" I yelled at him.

"That is what I'm trying to avoid," Vincent strangely replied. He nodded his head at the officer, who nodded back. "Good evening, officer."

Vincent took off down the pipe into the impenetrable darkness. "Couldn't we at least go back for a flashlight?" I pleaded.

"No."

I slumped down in his hold and crossed my arms over my chest. "You're impossible."

"I try."

"You succeed." I glanced over his shoulder at the retreating lights of the zombie's eyes. "Mind explaining what a zombie's doing as an officer?"

"They are nearly impossible to destroy, and they feel no pain when they lose an arm," he explained.

I cringed. "The retirement package must be pretty nice for them to take up that job."

"They are impressed into the service."

"How are they impressed with the service?"

Vincent sighed. "They are forced into being officers, or they will be destroyed."

"What kind of life is that?"

"Sometimes living is worth it."

I was struck by how sentimental that comment sounded. "Even if it means being a vampire?" I guessed.

He didn't deign to reply, and we made the rest of the journey in silence. It was a zig-zag route that ran us through wider and taller culverts until I felt we were in caverns. The angle of the floor led us down, and sometimes Vincent ran through water, but the caverns were relatively dry. Torches appeared on the walls and after a few miles we were joined by other people and creatures. There were a few other zombies dressed like Officer Romero, but most of the people were normal in their clothes and physical appearances. The other occupants appeared out of other tunnels that met at crossroads, and those crossroads met at other crossroads. It was a crossroads-topia that ended at a large terminal.

The terminal looked like one of those old-fashioned subway stations with the painted walls and high ceilings, but there was no natural light from above. We were still below ground, and large chandeliers lit up the space. The station had two levels with the second accessed via stairs on either end of the lower platform. The entire second level of the terminal was a towering business with several double-door entrances and a glass window atop them that reached to the curved ceiling. Shops lined all the walls on the ground floor that weren't open to tunnels, and their windows were filled with everything a ghoul could want from clothing to food.

Vincent let me down and led us up to that large establishment on the second level. Even before we reached the doors I could hear the sounds of slot machines and arguing. It was a giant casino, and the doors led onto the gambling floor. Four levels stood above us, all with balconies where people dressed in fine clothes watched and pointed at those who risked their money on the machines and cards.

Vincent strode through the gambling floor and to the rear where stood another pair of double-doors. Over these was a sign with the name Boo Bar in dripping red letters. "I wonder if they serve Bloody Mary's," I quipped.

"Quiet, or someone will hear you," he whispered.

I scowled at him. "So what? I didn't say anything wrong, did-ah!" Out from the wall to the right of the entrance slithered a giant eyeball complete with lashes and lid. It blinked and peered closely at us. I squeaked and hid behind Vincent. He glared at the eyeball and passed through the doors with me latched onto the back of his coat. When we were inside the dimly lit bar I glanced behind us and saw the eyeball emerge on the side of the wall beside the entrance.

I clung to Vincent's arm and was grateful when he didn't brush me off. My eyes were stuck on the eye. "M-mind explaining that?" I asked him.

"Yes."

With me closely attached to him Vincent wound us through two dozen low, round tables and past the bar that stretched long the left wall. I glanced around at the patrons and their spirits as they made jolly at the bar and at the crowded tables. Most of the bottles were full of the hard stuff. Vodka, bourbon, whiskey, and the like. What surprised me was how fast the customers consumed the alcohol, and all without any chasers. Hell, some of them downed straight vodka like they were taking tea. Any normal and sane person would have at least given a breather between swallows, but I had a feeling these people were neither normal nor sane.

Vincent's focus lay on a short man slumped against the far wall with one arm on the table by his chair. The stranger wore a hat with a large brim that covered his face. Ten yards away I could smell the scent of alcohol that wafted from his clothes. There was also a colorful splattering of dry puke all the way down his shirt. Vincent detached from me and smoothly slid into the chair on the opposite side of the table. That left me standing there like a scared idiot which is how I felt in this strange, terrifying place.

Vincent sat there for a few silent minutes until the drunk stirred. "Whadda ya want?" he slurred without lifting the brim of his hat.

"Information," Vincent

"Information?" The man hiccuped. "Don't got none, unless ya got some nice whiskey to be giving me."

"I have something better."

At Vincent's comment the man raised his head and I could see one attentive eye. "Better? What's better than a nice bottle of whiskey."

"Your life."

The eye didn't show any fear, but rather amusement. "My life? I already got one of those. Come back with a bottle of whiskey and we'll-"

"Tell me what I want to know or I will take your life," Vincent warned. There he went with that special diplomacy of his.

The stranger glanced over Vincent's cool, calm expression and must not have liked what he saw because Vincent was deadly serious. "We can't talk here. The eyes have walls." I frowned. Gone was the slurred speech and begging for whiskey. The man stumbled to his feet and out through a nearby door. We followed him, or at least I followed Vincent, and we stepped out into the rear of the casino. That turned out to be another underground hallway that branched off in a half dozen other passages. "How big is this place?" I asked them.

The evidently fake drunk glanced at Vincent and jerked his head over to me. His hat was raised so I could see he was human in appearance, but very pale. Even worse than Vincent. "Who's the noob?" he asked in the same clear, sober voice.

"No one of consequence, now tell me what I want to know," Vincent insisted.

The guy glanced down at my hand, and his face stretched into a wide grin. "She's your new partner, isn't she?"

"That doesn't matter," Vincent replied.

"It matters to me, and the rest of the world," the man argued. He jumped forward, grasped my hand and planted a soft hiss on my palm. "The name's Mitch Chaney, but you can call me anytime. A very great pleasure to meet you, and my condolences for your loss."

"Loss?" I repeated.

Chaney jerked a thumb toward Vincent. "If you hang out with him long enough you're going to lose your sanity."

Vincent's arm snapped out and he grabbed the man's collar. The vampire dragged him in front of him and lifted him a foot off the floor. "Tell me what I want to know about those who murdered Tim," Vincent growled.

"Hey, don't be ruffling up the suit!" Chaney yelped. I couldn't see how anything could make it any worse. Vincent didn't either, because he tightened his grip on the collar. The cloth wrapped tighter around the man's throat, and his voice came out in a choked whisper. "I'll tell! I'll tell!" he promised. Vincent dropped him onto his feet, and Chaney brushed off his suit and scowled at Vincent. "Yeesh, you sound like a broken record. Besides, I don't know much myself. Seems whoever knocked off your old partner did it real hush-hush. Don't know who, don't know where and don't know why, but I know his body's at the Third Precinct. Don't know how you're going to get in, but you might want to get that body before they decide he'd be real useful as a zombie."

Vincent's eyes narrow and he stalked off down the hall. I glanced between his back and Chaney. "Um, thanks for the help," I told him.

Chaney smiled and swept his hand over his chest in a bow. "My pleasure, Miss-?"

"Stokes," I replied.

"Miss Stokes. Never say that Mitch Chaney wasn't useful to you."

"I won't." I hurried after Vincent and caught up to him a quarter mile down the passage. Damn him and his speed.

"Um, mind explaining why we just talked with a guy who fakes his own sobriety?"

"Because in his act he hears and sees more than anyone would suspect," Vincent explained.

"And now where are we going?"

"To the Third Precinct."

"A police station?" The name sounded familiar.

"No. The Third Precinct is one of the larger warehouses for the Sanguine Syndicate."

Chapter 11

"You mean the people who've been trying to kill me since they killed Tim?" I asked him.

"Yes," Vincent replied. We wound our way through that maze of tunnels and the torches prevented me from eating pavement and sewer rat.

"Um, I may be dense-"

"Yes."

"-but shouldn't we be staying away from those guys?"

Vincent stopped so suddenly that I clothes-lined myself into his arm. I fell to the hard, cold ground, and he half-turned and glanced down at me. "Do you wish for your friend to be safe?" he asked me.

"Yeah, if he was alive, but he's not. Even that guy said he'd been murdered," I reminded him.

Vincent's frown deepened to the depth of the Grand Canyon, or maybe even a little lower. "Have you learned nothing?" he commented.

I stood and brushed myself off. "From what? Bits and pieces of information that I drag kicking and screaming out of your undead carcass? How the hell am I supposed to learn anything from that?"

He turned and strode toward me. I retreated until my back hit the wall of the tunnel, and he towered over me. His voice was low and dangerous. "You no longer exist in the human world. This is the world of the paranormal where morals are a dead-weight, and magic and science grant people their greatest wishes and nightmares. Life is created and nothing ends until the corpse is consumed by fire or the earth. We must retrieve Tim's body before they use their powers to return him to an existence they can use."

I cringed, not so much from the words but from the hideous warning in his voice. "What can they do to Tim?" I asked him.

Vincent pulled back and glanced down the tunnel. "We haven't time for the possibilities. That corpse holds memories that must not be revealed, and so it must be destroyed."

"Isn't there some way to save Tim's memories? You know, for good?" I wondered. Memories were what made us, and destroying those meant finishing Tim off for good.

"It would be too dangerous, but we've wasted enough time." He grabbed my hand and tugged me along down the tunnel. Nothing strange about that except my feet left the ground when he shifted from human to vampire speed. I yelped and grasped onto his arm with my free hand.

We sailed through the tunnels, zig-zagging our way from one dark passage to the next. I didn't doubt that this system went beneath the entire city, a subterranean subway system for the paranormal express. Vincent didn't slow down until well after my face was plastered with bugs and my hand was numb from his firm grip. This speed stuff wasn't all it was cracked up to be, and it definitely wasn't fun.

My feet touched the ground and I wobbled on my weak knees. "Isn't there some train or bus we can take?" I begged him.

"No." Vincent stepped up to a ladder, and I glanced up and saw a circular light that outlined another manhole. He climbed the ladder and left me to scramble after him. Vincent opened the heavy round door and disappeared into the clear night air. I followed, and saw we were one road away from the river and not too far from the warehouse where I'd met Vincent.

"I thought we were going to the Third Precinct?" I asked him.

"It's only a mile down the river," he replied.

"That close to your old hideout?"

"What better place to hide than beneath their noses?"

"Any place cleaner than beneath their noses."

Vincent ignored my snark and led me across the block to the riverfront. Only a worn dirt road separated us from the large rocks and trash that made up the bank. We kept to the shadows of the tall, brick industrial buildings that lined the waterfront and in a few minutes I spotted some activity along one of the buildings that lay on the other side of the river road. Vincent and I stepped into the nearest alley, and we both glanced around the corner at our target.

Our target was an island of boulders and gravel created in the days when river conservation meant keeping it open for traffic. On the island was a tall, square building with twenty floors and a flat roof. It was one hundred yards by one hundred yards square, and loomed over the old buildings on the opposite side of the road. Around the perimeter was a barbed wire fence several feet tall and tipped with spikes. The fence was open on the far side and a short flight of steps led down to several long docks that stretched out into the river. Between the building and the docks sat a half dozen large container trucks, and I noticed they were unloading the trucks onto the small boats on the docks. All but one of the craft were wide fishing boats most suitable for carrying cargo. The odd one was a jet craft with black paint and red racing stripes along the sides to make it go faster.

Guards with large, scoped guns and dogs on thick, black leashes patrolled every inch inside and outside the fence. There was a gap of ten feet from the edge of the island to the fence, and a gap of fifty feet from the fence to the building. The island was connected to land by a road that led along the fence to a rolling chain-link gate where sat two small guardhouses, one on either side. One of the black dock trucks exited the compound through the front gate and drove down the road away from us.

"Cozy place," I murmured.

Vincent slapped his hand over my mouth and his eyes wandered over the island. I didn't know how he thought we'd get in there unless he had a few magic tricks up his sleeve. The place was like Fort Knox on high alert. While Vincent tried his hand at infiltration I wrenched myself from his other hand and wandered down the alley away from the terrifying guns, dogs, and imminent death. I reached the end of the alley and peeked down the neighboring blocks. Far off in the direction we'd come I saw a pair of headlights that belonged to a vehicle like those in the compound. An idea struck me and I turned around only to collide into Vincent's chest.

His eyes looked in the direction of the vehicle that was barreling down the road toward us, and a twisted grin slipped onto his face. "Let me guess, you want to stow away in the back of the truck?" I spoke up.

"No."

"In the cab?"

"No."

"On top?"

"No."

"The grill? Tailgate?"

"No."

I paled. That left only the undercarriage. "Oh hell no."

"That may be our destination if this doesn't succeed."

"You're making that trip alone. I plan on going up on the elevator. Besides, how are we going to get under that thing with it moving? We'd have to do some epic sliding or-" The grin on his face widened. "You know, maybe I should stay here. I want to survive to see another sunrise, and even if this does work and we do get inside I'd just be a target for them," I pointed out.

"That is why you're coming," he told me.

My face drooped and I glared at him. "Thanks. Makes me feel so special, but I'm still not going." I held up the ring on my finger. "Unless this thing gives me the ability to make roads into slip-n-slides then there isn't any way you're getting-ah!" Vincent wrapped an arm around my waist and pressed me against him. I blushed and squirmed, and generally did a whole bunch of useless actions that tried to get me out of this trouble. Yeah, it all failed. "Let go! Damn it, I don't want to go!" The truck was fast approaching us.

"Not even for Tim?" he wondered.

I froze, and my eyes narrowed as I glanced up at him. "I hate you."

"Focus on that hatred and use it to stay alive."

"So I can what? Join the darksieee!" Vincent jumped out when the truck passed and pulled me onto his chest.

I clung to his coat as he slid down onto the road ten yards from the path of the truck. Our momentum sped us along and I closed my eyes when I saw we were headed toward the front passenger wheel. We avoided that squishy fate by a few inches and slid between the front and rear wheels. Vincent reached out and grabbed the muffler pipe, but the damn thing must have been made in China because it disintegrated in his hand. Fortunately, he latched onto another one of the doohickeys beneath the truck that I had no idea what it did, and that held. He lifted his legs and jammed them between the rear axle. Vincent pulled himself off the ground and me on his chest, so I was stuck between a rock and a hard place.

This was not fun. The road was bumpy, rocks and litter littered the street, and the ground zoomed below me like a spinning top of death. I clutched onto Vincent's chest and cursed his cursed existence. "This is not one of your better ideas," I yelled over the noise of the truck.

"So long as it works," he countered.

"That doesn't make it a good idea," I quipped.

The truck took the first right and drove down the driveway to the gate on the Island of Doom. It stopped for inspection at the gate. I held my breath and Vincent had the good fortune not to need to breathe as heavy boots walked around the truck. There were a few words exchanged and the truck lurched forward into the compound. It drove around the far side of the building to the docks and stopped.

Vincent dropped quietly to the ground and wrapped his arms around me so we were stuck face-to-face. This would have been romantic with the promise of a dinner and a movie afterward, but I expected shootouts and chases to ensue once we got inside. That was another problem we had to deal with before this rescue-corpse operation really got underway, getting inside. The driver jumped out of the truck and his heavy boots crunched against the gravel. Other boots joined his from the direction of the docks, and they unloaded the vehicle.

One of the guys was clumsy and dropped part of the shipment. A wooden crate fell to the ground and broke open beside the truck. Vincent and I got a good look at the contents, and it wasn't drugs and guns. Instead what fell out was books. Thick, hardcover books with strange symbols on the covers. I noticed Vincent's eyes narrow and his lips pursed together.

"Watch what you're doing! Those things are dangerous!" one of the men yelled.

I saw a man's hand come into view and grab at one of the open books. A dark light sprang from the pages along with a slithery, slimy tentacle. It grabbed the man's hand and yanked him down into the pages. I caught a good look at his terrified face and couldn't clap my hands over my ears hard enough to block out the terrible scream he cried before he was sucked into the book. Knowledge was not only powerful, it was terrifyingly strong and ugly.

"That's why ya gotta be careful!" shouted the first man.

The rest of the books were shut and picked up, but we still had other problems to deal with than possessed papers. Vincent scooted along beneath the truck toward the side of the building. I noticed a door along the wall, but it was closed and probably locked. I prayed for some way to get out from beneath this truck, and lo and behold but the door opened and a man in a gray business suit stepped out. The man was shorter than me, about fifty years old, and wore a pair of spectacles. I felt Vincent stiffen beneath me, but he didn't move. The strange man propped the door open with a heavy metal stapler and strode around the truck to speak with the work mules.

Vincent waited for the men on the right side of the vehicle to be deep in conversation with the new stranger before he rolled us both out from beneath the truck. He pulled me against him and sprinted over to the door. I hung there like a limp doll praying none of the guards would see us. Again we were successful, and I was starting to think this praying stuff really worked for me.

Chapter 12

Vincent hit the wall near the entrance and used me as a cushion. My shoulder knocked into the hard concrete and I glared at him. He ignored my look of love and opened the door to slide us inside. Once safely inside the very unsafe building he dropped me and we looked around the place.

We stood in a long, white hallway that was intersected by numerous perpendicular passages and dotted with countless doorways. It was a rat maze of white with our reward at the end being Tim's body. Voices floated down all the halls and the place was a beehive of activity. High-heels and boots clacked along the tiled floors.

Vincent slunk along the hall with his black coat blending in like a brown thumb at a Garden Party. I slunk along with him until we came to the first hall where he peeked around the corner to the front of the building. The new hall led to the lobby where we could just see the front desk with a bunch of people in police uniforms.

One of them looked very familiar, and I paled when I recognized Officer Sutton. That guy hadn't lied about bringing me down to the Third Precinct, but he deceived me about everything else.

I didn't have much time to wallow in my grumblings before Vincent grabbed my hand and yanked me in the opposite direction. The building stretched into the distance, but the structure was cut in half by a large dividing wall. Our hall stopped there, and turned off to the left and right, but not forward. The right passage took us to a dead end, and the left led to the center of the building. For all the busyness in the bustling building the halls we walked down were surprisingly empty.

The plain white halls gave me a headache and I was already disoriented. Then again, I got lost in walk-in closets. "Any idea where they keep the bodies?" I whispered to Vincent.

"No, but I don't believe think we'll-" Vincent yanked me down the right hall, pulled me against him and clapped his cold hand over my mouth.

I was getting real tired of him doing that to me, but at least it was for a good reason. The short, suited man from before strode up the hall behind us and took a left. He didn't look in our direction or he would have noticed us standing around the corner and in the open.

The little man walked twenty yards and took a right to disappear out of sight. Vincent released me and hurried after the stranger, and I hurried after him.

I misjudged my speed, probably because some ass didn't teach me how to control this new-found superpower, so when Vincent reached the corner I reached him just a split second later. We collided and fell onto the floor in a mass of legs, arms and, in my case, teeth. Vincent tried to roughly push me off and I bit his arm. He growled and smoothly slid out from beneath my flailing body. Somehow through all that madness nobody noticed us snooping around. I started to get the feeling that maybe this successful sneaking was a little too good to be true.

81

Vincent's pursed lips and narrow eyes told me something was up in his mind. I hated to do it, but I needed to find out what was going on in those rusted gears of his thoughts. "You get a bad feeling about this?" I whispered. He turned to me with a glare that silenced any more questions.

We heard a noise like a door latch, and both Vincent and I glanced down the hallway. The passage led into the other half of the building, and thirty yards down I noticed an open door on the left. Vincent hurried toward it and I followed behind him. We paused at the entrance and Vincent peeked his head inside. Vincent grabbed my arm and pulled me inside.

It turned out to be a coroner's office complete with silver-covered metal furniture and a door opposite the entrance that led to freezer in the back. Vincent led us to the rear room where we found metal drawers placed in a large wall. On the front of the square drawers were plates with words written on them. I shuddered and rubbed my arms to stay warm against the chill of the room.

Vincent stepped forward and his eyes swept over the plates. He started from the right and reached the middle when he froze at a drawer that stood waist-high. I stepped up beside him, and read the name plate. "Timothy Hamilton." The color drained from my face, and I looked to Vincent. "You really think it's him?"

"Only one way to answer that question," he commented.

We stepped to either side of the plate and Vincent pulled the drawer open. It slid out and revealed a frosted, semi-transparent bag that held something with the outline of a body. Vincent pulled down the zipper at the top and the bag split open to show a corpse of a man.

It was Tim.

I covered my mouth and turned away. I felt light-headed and the world spun around me.

My back hit the freezer wall and I shuddered. "Oh my god. . ." I murmured. Vincent unzipped the rest of the bag and drew Tim's naked body out of the freezer drawer. "We're really taking him with us?" I choked out.

"Unless you have the ability to transport him to another place," Vincent countered.

"Then at least find a sheet for him," I protested. His frozen parts were distracting me.

We found a white cloth close at hand and wrapped the blanket around corpse. Vincent hefted Tim's body over his shoulder, and the corpse lay stiffly against his back. I pushed off the wall and kept my distance from the grisly pair. We turned to the door, and found a new and frightening surprise.

The short, bespectacled guy stood in the doorway with a crooked grin on his face. "Good evening," he greeted us. His voice was soft, smooth, and creepy as hell. The man wasn't at all surprised to see us, and I realized why it'd been so easy to get into this place. So much for God's divine intervention.

Vincent's teeth ground together. "Get out of the way, Field," he ordered the short man.

"I'm afraid I can't do that, Vincent. Mr. Ruthven would like to speak with you." He glanced at me and I shuddered when those glassy eyes stared at me. "He especially wishes to meet you, miss."

"Ruthven will have to be disappointed," Vincent argued. He pulled Tim off his shoulder and tossed the corpse at our captor.

Field's eyes widened and he tried to move aside, but the body hit him in the side and they collapsed in a mess of stiff and squirming limbs. The man raised his head from the floor and Vincent knelt and punched him in the face. The man's glasses broke, and by the sounds of it so did his jaw. Field dropped to the floor unconscious, and I stood over them in shock.

"You threw Tim!" I yelled at him.

"It was a necessity," Vincent countered while he picked up Tim.

"How could you just toss him like a heavy popsicle?" I protested.

"With strength, now move," he ordered as he shoved me toward the hall door.

I led the way out into the passage, but we skidded to a halt when we noticed a group of armed guards coming at us from the front of the building. They were dressed the same as the ones from the warehouse, and with them were a half dozen men who wore police uniforms. I saw Officer Sutton among them. He didn't look happy to see me, and I sure wasn't happy to see him. Vincent and I shot down the passage in the opposite direction and came to a four-path crossroad. I opted for the left, and Vincent took the right.

I glanced over my shoulder and saw half the officers take Vincent and the other half follow me. I also noticed those with the police uniforms tore out of their suits as their bodies expanded and fur sprouted from their skin. Their eyes turned that familiar shade of predatory orange and their faces stretched while their mouths filled with razor-sharp teeth. Pretty soon I was being chased by a pack of werewolves with the men in black right behind them.

Now the formerly-uniformed cops were much faster and a lot more agile. They bounded down the hallway and lunged for me, their pointed, glistening claws sprayed out to tear me to shreds. I yelped and shifted into superhuman overdrive. My feet flew across the linoleum floors and I had the benefit of traction. Their claws clacked against the floor and they wasted a lot of energy using more claw than pad.

More speed didn't mean I left them far behind, or behind at all. The men in black couldn't keep up, but a few of the werewolves reached and dove for me. I decided to steal home base and slid down so they grasped air and sailed over me. They hit the floor and skidded to a stop, or tried to. Their claws tap-danced along the linoleum and the werewolves ended up slammed against the wall directly in front of me.

And that brings me to another problem I had. I was running out of hallway. There was one last intersecting hallway that ran from the front to the back of the building, but I spotted a door on the right past the perpendicular passage with a bright, beautiful sign above it that read *Exit*. A third problem I found was I had no idea how to put on the breaks with this superhuman speed. I'd always had a couch made of Vincent to stop me, and I didn't think these werewolves would oblige. Then I noticed the knob on the door and with a little bit of skill I snatched the handle and managed to turn it. The door swung open and I pulled myself inside.

I found myself at the bottom of a fire escape stairwell, and to my left was the exit door. I shoved it open, tripped the alarm, heard the door behind me crash open thanks to the werewolves, and to top it all off standing in front of me was one of the perimeter patrol guards with not one but two attack dogs. This just wasn't my night. Things got worse when the patrol guard loosed his dogs and they jumped at me. I stepped back inside and plastered myself against the wall to the side of the exit. The dogs raced past me and collided with the werewolves. That quickly turned into a mess of gnashing teeth and claws.

With both doors blocked I shot up the stairs with several patrol guards close behind. They were too slow to keep up, but the werewolves extracted themselves from their canine brethren and raced after us. I didn't get a chance to take a detour onto another floor and so found myself at the top of the stairs with nowhere to go but through the roof door. I flung myself out into the fresh night air with the werewolves in close pursuit.

Chapter 13

I ran over to the edge of the roof and leaned over the three-foot tall border. The drop was seventy feet down onto the hard ground, and even if the water had been close enough I probably would have killed myself in that tall a dive. The werewolves burst through the door and whipped theirs heads around.

They spotted me, so I did the only sane thing I could think of. I climbed onto the roof border and turned to my pursuers. "Don't come any closer!" I warned. They skidded to a halt and snarled at me, and I shuffled a little closer to the edge. Sweat trailed down my brow and my eyes kept flitting to the drop below me. "I'll jump, I swear!" Yeah, that was my plan. Pretend to be an aspiring suicide and hope they wanted me more alive than dead so they'd give in to my demands to leave safely.

The werewolves glanced at one another and evidently didn't take me seriously because they smirked and crept toward me. I cringed and glanced over my shoulder. It was a long way down, and I wasn't sure if I hated the long drop or the sudden stop.

Jump. I nearly fell off when that word erupted in my head.

"What?" I yelled at my brain. The werewolves paused, unsure if they wanted to munch on someone who yelled at herself.

Jump! That voice sounded familiar in an annoying sort of way.

"A moment, gentleman," a smooth voice spoke up. I turned my attention back to my pursuer in time to see the werewolves part, and through their midst strode a man.

He wasn't any ordinary man, he was drop-dead gorgeous. The stranger stood a little over six feet tall and wore an impeccable black suit. His long black hair was tied back and accentuated his pale skin. He had a dazzling smile and a pair of blue eyes that shone like a fresh, clean lake, but were a little icy from the mountain runoff. His face was thin, his nose just the right amount of sharpness, and he had long, well-manicured fingernails.

"I don't think you really want to jump, Miss-?" the man asked me.

"Cognito. I.N. Cognito," I quipped.

The man chuckled. "It's a pleasure to meet Nobody, but allow me to introduce myself. I am Lord William Ruthven." He gallantly swept his arm in front of him and bowed to me. I cringed back and nearly slipped. That was the name of the guy four-eyes wanted to take us to. He raised his head and glanced at me left hand. A smooth grin swept across his lips. "I see you're the new partner for our mutual friend, Vincent. By the way, where is that interesting gentleman hiding? My men seem to have lost him in the bowels of my building."

"Maybe he was flushed out with all the other crap," I suggested.

Lord Ruthven chuckled and slowly strode toward me. I eyed him wearily, and he held out his hands as a show of good faith. "You're very amusing, much like Tim. Perhaps you and I can have a short chat inside?" He was five yards away. Four. Three.

Jump now!

I glanced over my shoulder at the fall, and his lordship didn't like that. Out of the corner of my eye his appearance changed. His face twisted with fury and he lunged for me. I dodged his hand, and in doing so my feet slipped and I dove over the edge. My scream pierced the air as I fell through it. I tumbled end-over-end with the world around me spinning in wild, uncontrollable circles. The ground raced toward me and I shut my eyes a few seconds before I hit. Only I didn't hit.

A strong and familiar pair of hands wrapped around me and plucked me three yards from the earth. I snapped open my eyes and found myself hugged against a dark coat. My savior landed us on the ground, and I looked up to find myself staring into Vincent's dark eyes. I'd never been so relieved, or relieved at all, to see those pair of eyes, but now I wrapped my arms around his neck and hugged him. He stiffened and quickly set me on the ground.

"Stop wasting time. We haven't escaped yet," he reminded me.

Indeed we still stood beside the Building of Doom inside the Compound of Death with the Big Bad Guy staring down at us from the roof. Our position in the Compound of Death was on the far side of the building close to the docks. I turned my head and noticed a couple of stacked bodies in the shadows of the building. They were the patrol guards and their dogs, and they weren't moving. I didn't see Tim's body.

Vincent didn't let me sight-see any long when he grabbed my hand and dragged me in the direction of the docks. "What'd you do with Tim?" I asked him.

"Worry about yourself," he argued.

89

Above us I could see what he meant because the werewolves dove over the side of the building. They scraped their claws along the wall to slow their descent so they could drop around us. We ran along the building and around the corner. There was another truck unloading more wooden crates, and Vincent pulled me toward the men who were loading the boxes onto the boats. He pushed me toward the boats and dove at the workers. Vincent smashed his hand into the box carried by the men, and the wood splintered apart and books spilled out. The workers screamed and scrambled back, but their feet kicked open the hardcovers and stepped onto the pages.

Phantom, demon, tentacle and monster hands reached out and sucked the men into the pages like an erotica novel come to life. Vincent dodged all the fallen books but one. His foot slipped on the corner of a page, and a skeletal hand reached out and grabbed him. He fell to the ground and twisted around to kick at the creature. At the same time the werewolves rounded the corner and ran at both of us.

I sprinted over to Vincent and the books, and proceeded to lodge the whole box at our furry foes. The book pages hit them and the things inside the paper kept the werewolves preoccupied while I grabbed the cover of Vincent's book and slammed it closed. The bony hand fell lifeless to the ground, and Vincent yanked it off and tossed it against the nearby truck so it shattered into a million pieces.

I grabbed a spare book before Vincent grabbed me and hauled me to my feet. He led me to the river boats where a few of the men stood, not daring to risk the books to jump us. I held out my spare book, and they screamed and jumped into the water to escape the deadly paper cuts. We commandeered the speedy jet craft and Vincent steered us out into the water. He shifted to full throttle and I fell back into the rear seat. We sped off, and I glanced behind us at the shore. The werewolves still tussled with book demons, but on the docks we just left stood Lord Ruthven. We missed him by a split second, and from the furious look on his face I was glad we hadn't exchanged parting words.

We shot down the river and I slumped down in my seat. I flung an arm over my eyes and groaned. "Let's never do that again," I pleaded.

Vincent scoffed. "That is a normal night," he told me.

I raised my arm and looked at him with a horrified expression. "You're kidding, right?"

"No."

"For once can't you make a joke?" I begged.

"No."

We traveled in silence for a few miles and Vincent docked us on the lonely, quiet shore where we abandoned the boat for the cloak of the city. However, I refused to be carried like a damsel too feeble to put one foot in front of the other. He tried to pick me up, and I jumped out of his reach. "I can use my super speed just fine now," I argued.

"I haven't seen proof of this," Vincent countered.

"Probably because you went the wrong way."

"I escaped much quicker than you."

"I haven't seen proof of this," I shot back.

"Then where is Tim?" he asked me.

My face twisted into disbelief. "You didn't lose him, did you?"

Vincent rolled his eyes. "I had time to remove his body to a safe place and return for you."

"Oh. So you-so you came back for me?" I wondered. To be honest, even with our ring bond ruling us both I didn't think he'd go to so much trouble to save me.

He held up his ring. "I had little choice."

I crossed my arms over my chest and frowned. "Of course you had choices. You could have made me squirm up on that roof, or told me to jump and-" I paused and raised an eyebrow. "How did you tell me to jump, anyway? All I heard was this ringing voice in my head."

"Telepathy," was his bland response for a not-bland subject.

"Telepathy?" I repeated, and he nodded. I waved a finger back and forth between us. "So you're saying we can talk to each other without-well, talking?"

"Yes."

"Really?" I persisted.

"I will not lie to you," he returned.

My face broke open in a grin as I thought of the possibilities. We would perform at shows all across the country and show off our connection! We could make millions and retire to an exotic island where Vincent would probably end up turning into dust! All we needed to do was refine the act and-

A sudden, terrible thought struck me and I glared suspiciously at Vincent. "You can't *read* my thoughts, can you?" I asked him.

"No," he replied.

I mentally wiped my brow and dumped the idea of the millions. I was state-shy, anyway. "All right, so what do we do now?" I wondered.

"Now Tim's corpse must be destroyed."

My stomach fell and the color drained from my face. "How?" I squeaked.

"He wished to be cremated," Vincent told me.

I tilted my head and my face scrunched up. "Cremated? Isn't that kind of hard to do without a furnace?" Vincent's impatient reply was to turn his back to me and stride into the jungle of the city buildings. "Hey, wait!"

Chapter 14

I kept up, kind of. It was a lot easier running with superhuman speed on smooth, clean, even floors than it was over trashy, uneven streets filled with potholes the size of Buicks. The book in my hands didn't help, but I didn't want to drop it on the side of the road and doom a hobo to a grisly fate. Vincent led us back up the river toward the Compound of Doom, but veered onto several streets away from the water. We came to a bare lot with trash heaped taller than me, and in there he uncovered Tim's wrapped body where he'd hidden it beneath a bunch of clothes.

Vincent hefted Tim over his shoulder and I noticed the body wasn't as stiff and frozen. "We have to deal with this tonight, don't we?" I asked him.

"It cannot wait," Vincent replied. He glanced over me with a critical eye. "Can you run very far?"

I shrugged. "I don't know. Did this ring also give me a lot more strength?"

"Yes."

"Then I guess we'll see how far I can go."

Vincent turned away and sped along the streets, and I followed. We wound through commercial and industrial districts, houses and apartment buildings, and past the outskirts of the city. The hard road narrowed and the buildings became far and few. Corn fields replaced parking lots and large stores gave way to barns. I hadn't been out there except on joyrides, but I enjoyed what little I could see by the light of the stars above us.

Just when I thought I couldn't run any farther Vincent turned off onto a dirt road. It led up to an abandoned barn with stacks of dry hay in front of the large doors. He set Tim's body on the top of the stack and wandered into the barn. I noticed a few barn boards stuck out of the straw, and turned to Vincent when he emerged from the barn with a box of matches n his hand. "You guys were ready for this, weren't you?" I whispered.

"Yes." He lit a match and tossed it on the pile.

We both stepped back when the fire took to its food, and in a minute the hay was a bonfire of flames that licked at the sky. I glanced down at the book in my arms, and then to Vincent. "Should I burn this?" I asked him.

He looked to me, and took the book off my hands. I was glad for the less responsibility, but curious when he stuffed it away inside his coat. "Bat will be curious to see this," he explained to me.

"Oh, right." I didn't think I wanted to know anymore, at least not until it got me into trouble.

Knowing from movies how awful burning bodies smelled, I made sure to stay upwind of the smoke. Vincent and I silently stood beside one another and watched as the flames consumed Tim's body. It was a terrible sight to behold, but I couldn't look away. All the memories of the great jokes and laughs and teasing we'd had together went up with that smoke, and I felt a tearing inside me as I spoke a silent goodbye to my old friend. I didn't even notice I was crying until I felt the tiny droplets drip off my chin.

I rubbed my eyes to stop them, and Vincent glanced down at me. His face was dry. "Problems?" he wondered.

I snorted and managed a small smile. "Yeah, I'm human and these damn emotions are bothering me."

"Emotions tell you that you're alive," he countered.

I stopped my pawing at my tears and glanced up at him with a raised eyebrow. "That was strangely emotional for an undead guy," I commented. Vincent shrugged and turned away from me. I gave him a closer look. In the firelight I was reminded how handsome he was, and in the soft lines of his face I detected a hint-smidgen-possibility of sadness. "Could I ask you-"

"Yes," he interrupted me.

"Yes what?" I returned.

"Yes to your question."

I leaned in and narrowed my eyes. "You weren't digging around in my mind seeing what I was thinking, were you?"

"That's neither possible, nor anything I would care to do," he replied.

"Then what was I going to ask?"

"You were going to ask if I had a soul."

I blinked. "How'd you know that?"

"It was the first question Tim asked me." Vincent turned to me and looked me over. "He must have seen a lot of himself in you."

"So if you have a soul how do you manage to-well, to kill people?"

"My soul isn't like that of a human." He closed his eyes and chuckled. "Sometimes I even bring it out and look at it."

I took a step away from him. "Oookay, that's creepy."

"That's what Tim would say," he replied.

"And he was right." I glanced back at Tim's remains. The fire was hot enough I couldn't stare directly into the flames, but that meant there would be only ash left of him. "So, um, what do I do now?"

"You survive," Vincent answered.

"Will that really keep me busy for long?" I asked him.

"What do you mean?"

"I mean just surviving sounds boring. Isn't there something interesting Tim did? You know, to pass the time?"

"He had his occupation," he reminded me.

"Oh, right, the business." I crossed my arms over my chest and furrowed my brow. "I suppose it can't be any more dangerous than what we did tonight?"

"Not often."

"And it pays decently?"

"Quite often."

"And it'll keep me out of trouble?"

"Not likely."

I clapped my hands together and playfully pushed my shoulder into Vincent. He swayed and raised an eyebrow "Well, why the hell not?" I mused. "I've got a lot of time on my hands so I may as well take over his business. Besides, with you as an employee somebody else has to be the front-man for the customers. Otherwise they'll all be scared away." Vincent cracked a smile, and I wagged my eyebrows. "There, that's the look I want from a happy employee of-" I frowned. "Um, what did I just take over, anyway?" Vincent's face fell and he looked at me with an annoyed expression. I shrugged and sheepishly smiled. "Tim just told me he was some kind of consultant."

"Private detective," he blandly replied.

I blinked. "Private detective? That's what got him into so much weird trouble?"

"Paranormal private detective."

"Oh, that would explain you and-well, everything else."

"Yes."

"What's the name of this business?"

"Vampire Dead-tective Agency."

"Catchy."

"It was Tim's idea."

"It would be. So is this sleuthing business hard? Any special skills I need to learn?"

"Yes."

I waited with bated breath for further explanation. I nearly suffocated. "Mind telling me what they are?" I gasped.

"Experience is the best teacher."

"If you don't tell me something useful I'll stick voodoo pins in my own crotch," I threatened. Through our joined pain that would hurt him more than me.

"Diplomacy is useful," he spoke up.

"I prefer the more direct route of threats."

"So I noticed."

"It gets results."

"So I noticed."

I sighed and shrugged, but there was a mischievous smile on my face. "This is going to be a long, long relationship."

"Very long," he agreed.

And oh boy was it, particularly in that early adventure with the cult. . .

About the Author

A seductress of sensual words and a lover of paranormal plots, Mac enjoys thrilling reads and writings filled with naughty fun and pleasures. She writes stories in the paranormal and romance categories and always enjoys a good chat with fans and romance junkies.

You can find out more about her and her books at her website, *macflynn.com*, or through her twitter page at *twitter.com/MacFlynnAuthor*.

Printed in Great Britain
by Amazon